Archie and the Female Successors of Artross

Fay C Webb

Copyright Page

Published in 2008 by YouWriteOn.com

Copyright Text by Fay C Webb
First Edition

The author asserts the moral right under the Copyright, Designs and Patents Act 1988 to be identified as the author of this work.

All rights reserved. No part of this publication may be reproduced, stored in a retrieval system, or transmitted, in any form or by any means without the prior written consent of the author, nor be otherwise circulated in any form of binding or cover other than that which it is published and without a similar condition being imposed on the subsequent purchaser.

Published by YouWriteOn.com

This book is dedicated to

Katy, Lawrence, Christopher, Jessica, James, Elena, Edward and Percy.

My thanks go to Drs. Amanda Stuart and Chris Herring for their insights in the early days. Also to Diana Stewart, Sean, Bobbie, Jennie and the other children from Skipness, who read the early version of this story and gave me valuable advice which I have tried to incorporate into the final book.

Chapter One

Strange Happenings in the Old Lodge

It was still dark when Archie woke up, with a foul taste in his mouth and a dreadful smell in the air. Throwing the duvet aside, he leapt out of bed faster than he had ever done in his life, and shouted for his mum.

"Mum! The house is on fire!" he raced down the stairs, and nearly knocked his mother over as she came out of the kitchen, carrying some lighted candles, stuck onto saucers.

"Oops! Sorry Mum."

"All right, calm down Archie. The house is fine. We were hit by lightning last night. That's what you can smell."

"Wow! Cool!" enthused Archie.

"I'm glad you think so. Sorry to disappoint you, but there's no major damage. Now," she handed him a candle. There's no electricity, so you can take this candle up with you and get dressed. Be careful with it, and I don't want to see spilt wax everywhere. It's gone six thirty; if you don't hurry up you'll be too late to help Findley, he's waiting outside for you. Craig has already gone." Jimmy Mc Allister, who owned the newsagents, had promised Archie Craig's round. Craig was three years older than Archie and due to give up delivering papers to help in the shop, but that wouldn't be for another six months.

Archie groaned, in a demented moment he had agreed to help his friend Findley with his paper round every Saturday, as practice for when he had a round of his own. After a quick rub round his face with a flannel, Archie brushed his teeth, making faces at himself in the flickering candle-light. Then he quickly dressed, and finger brushed his hair upwards, into what he considered the coolest hedgehog style, and made his way down the stairs.

His mother, still in her dressing gown, met him in the hall. He handed her the sputtering candle.

"I'm surprised you slept through the storm last night." His mother said, "It was much fiercer than usual. I hope you switched your computer off before you went to bed, or your modem has probably been zapped. The phone lines are out, and with no electricity either, you will have to wait until they've been reconnected before you can check. I'm making a list of the damage later; the insurance company will want the details."

She drifted, distracted, into the kitchen, carrying the candle. Archie followed her.

"Why does the insurance company want to know?" Archie asked.

"They will replace anything destroyed by the lightning, like your modem, if it has been damaged."

"That's cool. Like Aladdin's lamp. New for old?"

His mother laughed. "You could say that I suppose."

"I'll try my modem tonight. I never heard a thing."

His mother looked at him and smiled. He dodged away as she attempted to ruffle his short black hair. "You would sleep through anything, Archie, now go on or you will make Findley late."

Archie grabbed a piece of cake and made his way out of the house to join his friend who was waiting for him just inside the gate.

Findley was at fourteen and a half, almost a year older than Archie, but the two had been firm friends since Primary One and got on very well together.

None of the street lights were lit, and it was very dark. Archie switched his bicycle lamp on.

"Hi Arch." Findley greeted him, "There's a terrible smell coming from your place. Like rotten eggs!"

"Sulphur." agreed Archie, sniffing, remembering his chemistry lessons. "It's probably from the storms last night."

"It stinks something awful. You're late," Findley continued, "I got tired of waiting and went to fetch the papers without you."

Archie nodded. "Okay, that'll save time."

They pushed through the gate together, wheeling their bikes down a rough stretch of road. Archie stopped.

"Can you hear that?" he asked Findley.

"What?"

"Sounds like a buzzing, it's getting louder. Where is it coming from?"

Findley shrugged, "It's coming from behind the hedge. Maybe the storm knocked a beehive over."

Archie's home was the last house on the estate, built many years ago on a large tract of land, belonging to the lord of the manor. The Big House had long since been converted into apartments, but the old lodge remained, next door to Archie's house. The old dowager had lived there. Now, many years after her death, the lodge had fallen into disrepair. The gardens were a thick tangle of brambles and weeds; and the whole place was surrounded by thick hedges and trees.

Archie, who had often played in the old place when he was younger, disagreed. "I don't think there are any bees there. At least, there never used to be."

"Well it's too dark to do anything now. We'll be late with the papers if we don't get a move on."

"Just a minute," Archie argued, "It won't take a sec, to have a quick look."

"All right then. I suppose a couple of minutes can't hurt."

Findley laid his bike down alongside Archie's against the hedge, and pushed the papers in behind them. Together they began to push their way into the lodge garden. Long grass grew through the bars of the rusty gate.

"Whew! This is hard work," panted Findley, "Nobody's been here for ages. The way in is almost completely blocked with brambles and bracken. Ouch!" he exclaimed, hastily tearing his glove off and sucking his fingers.

They had managed to partly open the gate and were about to slide through, when Craig, Archie's brother, rode up.

"Archie! Haven't you gone yet? What are you doing? You're late. When you take over my round, you'll have to do better than this. You'd better get a move on. I've finished my deliveries, and I'm going in for some breakfast. I'll see you back here later."

Archie called after Craig as he rode off, "Tell Mum I won't be home for breakfast. See you later."

Craig stopped pedalling, and looked back at his brother. "Archie! Don't you stay out all day. You're helping me at school this afternoon, and you'd better be there!" he shouted, as Archie and Findley hurriedly worked at the gate and shoved their way into the overgrown garden, anxious to avoid any further awkward questions.

When they were inside the garden, safely out of sight, Archie stopped. He sighed. Some time ago, one of the senior students had had the bright idea of inviting time travellers from the future to travel back in time to the school for a rendezvous on Saturday June 30th at 4pm. That day was today. The past few months had been taken up with preparing and burying such things as time capsules etc. They even organised radio and television presentations, and newspaper advertisements encouraging people to bury the details in their gardens hoping centuries into the future they would be found and acted upon.

Naturally anybody purporting to be from the future would have to bring proof, such as knowing the cure for the common cold, or cancer. Archie turned to Findley,

"Bother! I had forgotten all about the school project. Now I'll have to turn up, or I'll never hear the end of it from Craig."

"I shouldn't worry, Arch. There's bound to be nothing happening. Waste of time if you ask me."

"Right you are. Anyway, I'm more interested in what's going on here." he quickly pulled out his mobile and sent his brother a text.

"Meet u at school at 4. Ok?"

"There, that's done." he said, putting his phone back in his pocket. He looked around. "It's getting lighter now, Fin. We've got time for a quick look eh?"

"Well..." Findley was unsure, "We really ought to do the papers first."

"No way, we're here now, so let's go for it! Listen, that noise is getting louder."

Findley was reluctant, fearing the newsagent might sack him. "I'll wait here for you. If you're not back in ten minutes, I'll do the deliveries and then meet you back here."

"Come on, I thought we were mates. We've got plenty of time to do the papers later." Archie argued.

Findley was still unconvinced. "There's a new delivery today. The new house, you know; the one behind the lodge, in Hermian Lane. There used to be a passage from the back of this garden, that came out at the back of the estate. It's on your list. You could do it now, and then do the others later if you like."

"No." Archie was definite. "We'll do them all later. If anyone makes a fuss, we'll tell them we couldn't find the new house."

Findley knew when he was beaten. He shrugged. "Okay, but if things go pear-shaped, you can explain."

"Okay, okay." Archie was impatient to be tracking down the source of the sound. Although the sun was just beginning to lighten up the sky, there was an odd pink mist, hanging about in clumps. He'd noticed it before, on his way to school in the week, and was more than ever sure that something odd was going on.

He knew the house in Hermian Lane that Findley was talking about. He had discovered it last Saturday at the end of the round. He was astonished to see it, because he couldn't ever remember seeing it before and he'd taken the opportunity to have a quick snoop round.

The house had a strange feel to it that made him feel uneasy. Everything had been spotless. Painted a brilliant white, with black window frames, the house, built at the end of a huge length of grass, had appeared to frown; as if he was an unwelcome visitor. The white gravel drive had seemed untouched. He had noticed an archway leading round to the rear, and going through, had discovered the garages, built at the back.

He had gone up to the front door and listened, waiting for a few moments, but the house had been utterly still and silent.

Archie shivered, quickly shrugging away the memory of the strange house.

"What are we waiting for?" he demanded, and the two friends started to push their way further up the weed infested path, towards the lodge.

Archie noticed the pink mist was here again, hanging about in soft clumps that touched his face. It felt quite spooky.

As they moved through the high grass; the overgrown brambles clung to their legs, impeding their progress and slowing them down. The mist surrounded and moved along with them, preventing them from seeing further than a few feet in front, even though the sun was now quite high in the sky.

Everything dripped incessantly, and soon they were uncomfortably wet and wondering if this was such a good idea. Suddenly Archie heard an annoyed squeak, and scuffling, as a huge rat turned round and sat and stared at them. He quickly kicked out at the horrible thing, but it was totally unconcerned, moving slowly to one side, calmly watching them pass.

"Urgh!" Findley shuddered and hurried on as best he could.

Glancing quickly back over his shoulder Archie realised the rat they had seen, was only one of several. Their red eyes glowed, reflecting what little light there was. He loathed rats. His attention was caught by the sound of the buzzing. He stopped.

"Where's that noise coming from now? Fin?" he asked, trying to pinpoint if it was coming from the lodge or the new house beyond it.

"I can't make it out." Findley stopped and looked around. "It seems to be all around us now." he shivered, "I'm cold, and wet. I'm not sure this is such a good idea Archie."

Although eleven months older than his friend, he usually deferred to Archie's stronger character, but he wasn't too keen on places overrun with rats.

"I know, I'm soaked through too, but we're here now, so we might as well have a proper look round."

Findley said "I wondered if Murray might want to come out with us today, I tried to call him, but he hadn't switched his mobile on yet."

"Probably not up yet, lazy devil." Archie laughed.

Findley agreed. "I texted him. He may turn up later, you never know with him."

Privately, Archie hoped Murray would not bother. He had loads of time for his stepbrother, but he knew Emmaline would insist on coming with him. Although they were twins, Archie and his sister Emmaline had never got on well after they were split up when attending High school. It saddened Archie when he remembered the good times they had had when they were younger. They had invented their own language, used solely between themselves. Even their parents hadn't been able to interpret them. He didn't understand why Emmaline had been determined to go her own way. At least he and Craig were able to have their own rooms after she decided to live with their father after their parents split up. Archie and Craig lived with their mother, but they regularly saw their father, who had married Murray's mother. Findley interrupted his woolgathering.

"Hey Arch! You know what? This place smells just like yours. It stinks actually."

"Yes. Phew! It's pretty bad. It's probably left over from the storm last night. Mum said we had been hit by lightning. The phones don't work and we've got no electricity. Mum's been trying to sort things out, I got out, fast! That reminds me." Archie took out his mobile and switched it off.

He grinned at his friend "If they can't call me, I won't get carted back to help!" He pocketed his phone, and as he spoke, the remnants of the pink mist lifted suddenly.

"Hey!" Archie whispered. "Look Findley. There's the old lodge. It looks as if it's about to collapse! Emmaline and I used to play here, must be..." he thought for a moment, "At least six years ago. It wasn't as bad as this then."

The upper part of the roof was shrouded in the mist that had followed the boys from the path, but they could clearly see the house was uninhabited.

Findley grinned, "Come on. We can always say we were checking the house for damage done by lightning."

They threaded their way through the last of the tall grass to a small paved area, which the boys followed round to the back. The little cottage crouched low, under a thatched roof, black with age. Wild plants had established themselves comfortably in the gutters and on the windowsills. Birds flew in and out of the underside of the thatch.

The boys attempted to see in through the windows, but the glass was obscured by dust and dirt and their reflections stared back at them.

"Can you see anything?" asked Findley.

"No, come on, let's try at the front." As they made their way around the old cottage, the boys could hear the buzzing again.

"It's coming from inside." Archie said as he pulled at the creeping ivy covering the porch, and tugged open a dilapidated screen door. It fell apart, and insects scurried for cover. The boys slowly crept onto the porch, and then stopped, each waiting for the other to make the first move.

Findley, his red hair standing on end, and his eyes alight with mischief stepped forward. As he touched the front door, it slowly swung inward. He stopped, startled. "It opened before I touched it." he stammered.

Archie pushed him. "Don't start! I saw you shove it. Come on!" he stepped inside boldly, followed by a subdued Findley.

"Watch your feet, the floor could be rotten. Better stand still for a minute; let our eyes get adjusted. Wow. It's really dark in here."

Findley walked carefully round the edge of the room until he reached a window. "No wonder we couldn't see in the glass. There's a blind covering it." As he reached over to it, the blind sprang up; Findley stepped back abruptly.

"It did it again!" he muttered.

Bright sunlight flooded the room; there was a sound almost like a sigh; and the small cottage seemed to tremble.

Archie and Findley stared at one another for reassurance.

Findley whispered, "Did you feel that?"

"It's just the house relaxing!" said Archie, trying to convince himself. He looked about. Everything was covered in dust and thick cobwebs were strung across the walls and hung low from the light fittings. Clouds of dust rose from under their feet at every step they took.

"Nobody has been here for years. Hey! That's weird!"

"What?" nervously breathed Findley.

"Archie pointed to the floor. "Look Findley, that bit of carpet; it's perfectly clean!"

In the middle of the large moth-eaten and dusty carpet there was a roughly circular area, almost a metre across, which was absolutely clean. The coloured patterns of the silks were clear and bright, contrasting like glowing jewels with the rest of the carpet. The humming, buzzing sound suddenly increased in volume as Findley and Archie knelt down and examined the clean patch on the old floor covering.

"That's very strange. It's not marked at all," said Findley wonderingly, as he trailed his fingers across the clean surface. He looked around at the rest of the room, "What is this? You can see nobody has been in here for ages, the only footprints are ours."

Archie nodded. "It's pretty weird. Something must have been standing here until recently. Not heavy though. There aren't any marks."

Findley stood up and sniffed, puzzled. "Archie, can you smell that?"

"Yes, it's the same as on the path. It's the smell of the lightning again, but its bright sunshine now."

As he spoke, the brilliant light streaming in at the window was suddenly blotted out. Archie and Findley swung round and stared. A face with a hand cupped either side was peering in at them.

"Oh! It's only Murray," Findley sighed in relief, his heart hammering. "You gave us a scare Murray. Come round the front, the door's open." he shouted.

Murray mouthed something, but they could not hear what he said. They waited a few moments, but there was no sign of him.

"Let's have a quick look around the rest of the house, and then we must get back and deliver the papers. Murray's probably got sidetracked. Findley urged.

"Okay." Archie agreed, "There's nothing much to see here anyway."

As they moved together towards the door, it slowly swung closed, and then, with a loud click, it locked.

"Hey! What's going on? Open the door! Murray! This isn't funny." Archie shouted. He wrestled with the handle for a few moments, but it was locked fast.

"It's no good Findley, I can't open it, you have a go..." he turned, shocked. Findley had disappeared.

"Findley? Where are you? What are you playing at? The door is locked and we're trapped."

Archie looked quickly round the room, moving carefully, searching behind the silent pieces of huge furniture that stood covered in dustsheets, lifting them slowly to look underneath.

Nothing seemed to have been disturbed. Finally, he had to acknowledge his friend was not hiding anywhere in the room. "It must be some trick." he said out loud. His voice echoed around the silent room, and made him jump.

Ten minutes later, Archie was getting extremely anxious. Again he attempted to open the door, and to his utter astonishment, it opened easily. He turned to give the room one last look, holding the door firmly in his hand. He nearly jumped out of his skin with shock. Findley was standing directly behind him.

"What the hell are you playing at?" he shouted, his sheer relief turning quickly to anger. "Where have you been?"

"What on earth are you on about? I haven't been anywhere. I've been right here with you."Findley exclaimed.

"I've been looking for you for the past ten minutes!" Archie explained about the door locking itself.

"I never saw it lock!" Findley argued. "I certainly haven't been hanging around for ten minutes either. You're losing it mate!"

"Now you just listen to me! Look Findley." Archie had calmed down. Quietly he added "There is definitely something weird about this place, I mean really weird. I swear to you, you disappeared for ten whole minutes. I searched this room, then the door unlocked itself." In his hurry to explain to Findley what had happened, Archie let go of the door, which immediately began to swing shut again.

"Quick! Catch the door!" Findley shouted as the door closed behind Archie. "Oh, oh, too late."

Archie groaned. "Now what?"

"Hold on a minute, Arch. I just thought of something." Findley caught his friend's arm. "Did you step onto that clean piece of carpet?"

"No." said Archie surprised "Why would I? Oh," he said "Did you?"

"Yes." Findley answered him. "Well, I sort of hovered, you know? I just put half of one foot in at the edge."

"What happened?" asked Archie.

"That's just it. Until you said about me being missing, I didn't think anything had."

They looked at each other, silent, thinking...

"We're trapped." Archie said finally. "We'll have to get out of the window, it looks as if it's about to collapse anyway."

Both boys went over to the window, and Archie tried to open the catches. After struggling for a few minutes and getting more and more frustrated, he stood back. "It's no use," he said, "It's stuck fast."

Findley, out of the corner of his eye thought he saw movement behind him. He swung round, "Murray!" we wondered...."

"What?" asked Archie turning back from the window.

"I thought I saw Murray," said Findley, bewildered. "I swear it was him, but he's just disappeared!"

Now who is being pathetic?" scoffed Archie. "Come on. Let's have a proper go at this window." He looked about the room. "If we can find something to hit it with," he said, "We could break the glass. See if there's a poker or something."

"There is only this," said Findley, handing Archie a heavy brass toasting fork. "It was in the fire-place. I can't find anything heavier."

"It will have to do then. Give it here." Archie took the proffered toasting fork, and gave it a hefty swing, aiming it at the glass. As he did so an extraordinary thing happened. The fork bounced out of Archie's hand before it could hit the glass. He picked up the fork and tried again, with the same result. He became angry, and gripping the fork firmly, he tried a third time, really putting his weight behind as he swung at the window. The same thing happened.

"Oh, come on Archie!" sighed Findley, "Give it to me. I'll have a go." He took the fork from Archie and hammered at the window. The fork jumped out of his hand.

"I don't believe it," he said picking up the fork from the floor and examining it closely. "Strange. It looks quite ordinary." He put it back in the fireplace. "It's no good, Archie; the house doesn't seem to want us to leave."

"This is crazy," said Archie. I know there's no other way out. I searched this room from top to bottom when you were missing. Let's try the door again." he tried the handle, but it wouldn't move, he shrugged.

"Guess what? This is ridiculous." snorted Archie. He thought for a few moments. "Listen, Fin, if half of your foot touching that clean patch on the carpet moved you for ten minutes, it must be another way out."

Findley laughed nervously.

"Look Fin, the worse that can happen is we'll still be standing here feeling stupid,"

Archie coaxed the reluctant boy. "Come on. Let's have a go. I don't want to be stuck here all day."

He grasped his friend's belt. "That's it hold onto my belt. Ready? Right then, now!"

Together, Archie and Findley stepped onto the pristine surface of the carpet. Immediately they were aware of a loud buzzing sound.

"There's that noise again!" Archie grabbed Findley's shoulder as he was overcome by a strange lassitude. Feeling extremely dizzy, Findley leaned towards Archie as if he was about to speak; when he felt a huge gust of wind and he realised he was being pulled upwards. As he opened his mouth to shout he fell into a deep sleep, a second later, Archie was asleep too.

He dreamed he was in the middle of a green field, bathed in a blinding white light. He opened his eyes slowly, and remembering the strange happenings in the lodge that morning, he realised he was not dreaming at all. He and Findley had escaped from the room all right, but had ended up here, wherever 'here' was.

The strange sound he had heard when they stepped onto the clean patch of carpet was still humming away, but it was quieter. He thought it seemed to be coming from the ground. His tongue felt huge, and swollen in his mouth, and he was dying for a long cool drink.

He tried unsuccessfully, to lick his dry lips. Looking around for Findley, he found him lying on the grass, a short distance away from him. He was still asleep. Archie sat up. Somehow they had arrived out in the open air, landing on the strangest grass Archie had ever seen. It was most unusually soft, and a vivid green colour. It extended to ten square metres, beyond which there was nothing at all, just a shimmering rainbow coloured wall surrounding them. Looking up, he could see it stretched right above them, and it was filled with an extremely bright light.

"It's a soap bubble, but it's huge." Archie thought. "And we're inside it. Findley!" he said urgently, "Wake up!" he shook his friend roughly. "Look! Look where we are!"

"Where are we?" Findley said sleepily.

"I don't know. I think we are in some kind of bubble. The walls don't look very thick to me." Archie stood up. "Get up, Findley, we must try and find a way out."

Findley got to his feet, staring around him. Together, they drew near to the sparkling, rainbow walls.

"It's wet!" said Findley awed, running his hands over the surface. "It moves when you push it." His hands made an impression in the silky lining of the bubble, and sprang back into shape when he removed them.

"It is a bit like wet cling film, but much stronger," said Archie."Have you noticed there are no edges? It's just like a huge, see-through mushroom."

"It is except you can't see through it!" Findley argued. "It is so bright in here. The light is hurting my eyes."

After several minutes of poking ineffectually at the shimmering walls, the boys sat down to consider their predicament.

"Try your mobile, Arch." Findley suggested, pulling his own out of his pocket. "That's funny!" he said as he looked at it closely. "This is dead. I only charged it last night." He looked over at Archie, "What is yours like?"

"Weird, mine is completely dead too." Archie shrugged and put his mobile back in his pocket.

"Where do you think we are Archie?" asked Findley, "I don't know about you but I've got a nasty feeling we've jumped from the frying pan into the fire. How are we going to get out of here?" He punched the walls of their enclosure in frustration. He idly ran his hand through the grass, and bent his head to take a closer look at it. "I've never seen grass like this before, have you? Look."

He attempted to pick a blade of grass, but was surprised to find how difficult it was. "Wow. It's a lot tougher than it looks. Uh!" the grass suddenly snapped in his hand, and he snapped another. "These are quite short, like a mown lawn, but there's no cut edge!"

He picked several more pieces, and said in astonishment, "They are all exactly the same. Even the shading is in the same place on each blade, Archie. Look at this! They're clones!"

Archie examined the grass in Findley's hand. "We've been learning about genetically modified crops at school. I suppose this is what they meant."

Findley shook his head. "No. This grass isn't your usual grass. It's like it's been made new altogether. It's very different from any we know."

Archie was no longer listening; his attention was caught by something outside their bubble. "Sssshhh!" Archie grabbed Findley's arm. "Look!"

Findley looked up at the wall where he could see claws trying to rip through the wall from the other side.

Chapter Two

A New Dimension

"What is it?" he whispered.

"I don't think I want to find out." Archie said softly.

The boys sat down in the middle of the grass, as far away from the walls as possible. They huddled together and watched, horrified as the claws repeatedly tried to gain entrance. Round and round the bubble, the creature prowled, trying hard to find a way in, as the boys watched, fascinated and fearful. Quickly they both ducked down flat as the animal sprang suddenly onto the top of the bubble. They could plainly see it outlined against the bright light outside, on the surface above them.

"It looks like a rat, but it can't be, it's massive. It is big as a horse!" whispered Archie "Stay quite still, Fin!"

"Do not worry, my friend. I am not moving an inch! Actually, I don't think it can get in." he added.

"And we can't get out!" said Archie as the creature jumped off, and the bubble resumed its original shape. "Phew! Whatever that was, it seems to have given up."

"Given up for now maybe, Archie. What is this place? How are we going to get out?" Findley was beginning to panic. "What are we going to do? I'm scared. Should we try shouting, see if we can make somebody hear us? But what if that animal comes back?"

Archie was about to attempt to quiet Findley's fears, when he noticed a bulge appearing in the side of the canopy wall. "Quiet. Look!" he whispered, pointing at the wall.

Clinging to each other, they watched, fearful as the bulge grew larger, and before their scared eyes, it gradually detached itself from the wall, changing as it glided smoothly towards them, into the shape of a young girl.

She appeared to be about thirteen or fourteen years old, with long, straight blonde hair surrounding an oval face. She had bright blue eyes; a turned up nose and a wide smiling mouth displayed very even white teeth. Her skin was the colour of milk chocolate, and she was dressed in a simple long sleeved tunic; in a mix of purples and grey. She moved gracefully towards them. They could see her entire body and clothes were covered in a layer of the same shimmering material as the wall.

Her mouth opened and she seemed to be speaking, but the boys were unable to hear her.

They scrambled to their feet and stared at her. Suddenly, they were startled to hear a tinkling laugh.

"Sorry. We communicate by thought transference. I believe you know it as telepathy. Your minds are unaccustomed, I think. Be careful with your thoughts; you must learn to contain them, and direct only what you wish me to know towards me. I have unlocked part of your brains. It will enable you to convey your thoughts. I will leave you now, to learn this skill together. When I return I will bring you some refreshments. I understand you are thirsty."

She smiled again, turned and silently stepped through the rainbow wall. The boys watched her leave with wondering disbelief.

"Did you hear that?" Findley was shocked. "She said she had unlocked our brains!"

Archie nodded. "Yeah right!" he thought. He said "Okay. Let us see if we can do it Findley. I'll think something, and you tell me if you get it." Archie stared hard at his friend.

Findley grimaced "Ouch! Not so loud, Arch! You are going to ask that girl what her name is."

"Sorry," thought Archie "You got it right. Now you think of something to say to me."

Findley thought "That is a lot better. Where do you think this place is?"

Archie thought back, "I don't know but it's seriously off, if you ask me. We'll find out when the girl comes back. Hey! We can really do this Findley. It'll be brilliant when we get back to school."

They laughed together, pleased with the idea of fooling their friends, and for a short while they amused themselves communicating without words, when suddenly, Archie gasped in shock.

"What's up Arch?" Findley said out loud, forgetting to direct it as a thought.

"I just thought..."

Findley laughed "Yeah, great innit?"

"Shut up a minute. Don't be a wally all your life. This is scary... Do you think, I mean. Could all this..." he waved his arms around. "Be anything to do with our school Future Project?"

Findley considered. "No. I shouldn't think so. This is too far out. Nothing is going to happen at school tonight...waste of time, if you ask me."

"Yes, you said that before, but you have to agree mate, this is way beyond normal." Archie was less sure, "I just wish I knew where we are."

Findley thought "I'm more bothered about getting out of this bubble, or whatever it is."

As he watched, the girl silently reappeared. She was carrying a tray, balancing three glasses and a jug containing a clear sparkling liquid. She sat down on the grass, next to the boys, placing the tray down beside her. She began pouring the liquid into the glasses.

"What is that?" asked Findley, remembering to send the query as a thought.

The girl laughed silently, but the boys could quite clearly hear her. "You have learned quickly. This is water." she added, as she passed each of them a glass.

She began to drink, watching them as Archie took a cautious sip. "It's delicious, Fin," he thought, "Try it. It is the best water I've ever tasted." He swallowed it down, revelling in the relief it gave to his dry mouth.

Findley tried his drink. "It's brilliant, it tastes. I dunno...Clean!"

"Yes." Agreed the girl as she quickly finished her drink and stood up.

"Are you leaving us again?" Archie asked her, as he scrambled quickly to his feet. "Who are you? What is this place? What was that animal that tried to get in?"

The boys heard her laugh again. "So many questions; my name is Heyke, and I am your guide for as long as you are here. I will take you outside and show you where we live. As for the animal," she paused, "It was probably a raptorvor. There are many animals here, which may appear strange to you. They have evolved on the surface in many different ways. Don't worry about them; in daylight they're much more scared of us than we are of them."

"That's a matter of opinion." thought Findley.

"It was most definitely a giant rat, then." Archie said.

"You must finish your water first," she added as Findley put his half full glass down on her tray. "It is important, because you will be unable to pass through the screen until you have absorbed something of our time into your bodies."

"Our time?" Archie asked her.

"This is the ninth dimension, and the screen will only allow you through when it recognises something from our time."

"What is the screen made of?" Findley asked, downing the rest of his drink so fast, he gave himself hiccoughs. He stood up and placed his hands on the wall. "It's so strong, yet it's wet!"

"I can see you have many questions. I will try and explain. The wall is a security and biohazard barrier. That means it prevents viruses and undesirables from other times invading our dimension."

Archie walked over to them at the wall as Hyeke was explaining to Findley.

"I would like to see where you live, but I don't understand what you mean by dimension. We are in the year 2008 in the twenty-first century. How can we be in a dimension?"

Hyeke laughed. "Let me see. Do you know what an onion is?"

"Yes." They thought together, picturing the mundane vegetable in their heads.

"Oh good. You can see it for yourselves."

Archie gasped "Can you see in our heads as well?" he demanded.

"Oh yes." answered Hyeke dismissively. "Now, let's get back to the onion. If you cut it in half, from top to bottom, you see it is made up of several segments, held together only at the root. Each segment is kept entirely separate from its neighbours by a thin film. This keeps all the segments independent from each other."

"Except at the root." thought Archie.

"Even at the root, there is no way any segment can touch another." Hyeke argued.

"So if one goes bad, the others are okay?" Findley suggested.

"Something like that." Hyeke agreed.

"What has all this to do with dimensions?" Archie asked irritably. He wanted to get out of there.

"Dimensions are how we measure time," Hyeke answered. "Time is a little bit like an onion. It has many segments. We call them dimensions. Each dimension is separated by..."

"Onion skins!" Findley giggled.

"Not exactly," Hyeke grinned. She was enjoying herself. "It's more like a thick net made up of various frequencies of radio waves. Do you know about those?"

"Yes." nodded Archie.

"Then you must know that radio waves never degenerate, so they make an ideal barrier."

"How did we get here then?" Archie wanted to know.

"Sometimes an earthquake or a fierce electrical storm can disrupt things, creating tears in the barriers, leaving a way through from one dimension to another."

"We had a huge electrical storm last night. It hit Archie's house. Didn't it Arch?" Findley interrupted.

"There you are then." Hyeke nodded.

"So this tear would make it possible to get to this dimension, from any of the others?" asked Archie.

"Not usually." Hyeke replied. "The radio waves are simply reformed into a long funnel, with no way to enter any dimension it may pass through. The funnels link dimensions by sheer chance."

"Does that mean every time there's an earthquake or a bad storm, a new funnel is made? There must be loads of funnels to other dimensions." Archie wanted answers.

"It doesn't happen every time. I only know of a few others. You are the first visitors I've seen for some time." Hyeke told him. "Most tears heal themselves very quickly."

"Hey! That means we will get stuck here!" Findley's thoughts reached them, sharp with fear. "How will we get back?"

"You need have no worries about that. When we leave this area, the barrier will extend itself down to the beginning of the funnel, keeping it open for your return. Now, are you ready?" Hyeke put her hand out towards the shimmering wall.

"Could you just tell me?" Archie wondered slowly,

"If this dimension is the ninth dimension, which one have we come from? And how many years does one last?"

"They all vary," Hyeke told them. "Some last for a few years, others last several millenniums."

"So we have travelled up the funnel a long way into the future?" Archie asked.

"Yes." nodded Hyeke.

"Where from? I mean which dimension was...is our time in?" he added quickly.

Hyeke paused, considering. "Hmm, the twenty-first century? That would be the second or maybe the third."

Reaching into a pocket, she brought out three dark plastic looking bands. She placed one across her eyes, and the startled boys watched as the band adjusted itself to her face, and rested above her ears. She handed the boys a band each.

"Take these now, and position them over your eyes as I have. They will protect you from the bright light outside."

Tentatively, the boys obeyed, amazed that the material adapted itself to the shape of their faces.

"Wow! These are class!" Findley enthused.

"Yes." agreed Archie. "You can hardly feel you've got them on. What a difference to the light. I can still see clearly, but much more easily now."

After ensuring the boys had put their eye protectors on properly, Hyeke touched the rainbow canopy. Her hand went through and disappeared. She stepped through the wall, carrying her tray, turning as she did so, requesting that Archie and Findley follow her. They hurriedly obeyed, hardly daring to believe this was actually happening to them.

As they walked through out of the other side, Archie could see Hyeke was clear of the shimmering barrier, but the material from the shield was still clinging to himself and Findley.

"How can we get this stuff off?"

"You can't," she replied. "It will stay on until you return to you own time. It will protect you." she added, "It prevents anything harmful entering your skin. It's just a precaution. Your bodies do not have the same level of protection as ours."

"It's not so uncomfortable," Findley thought. "At least it's dry now."

Archie forgot about the barrier material, as he looked round properly for the first time. There was no sign of the animal that had tried to get into the bubble.

He could see row upon row of identical buildings, set in the same green grass, which appeared to extend as far as he could see. There were no gardens, plants or trees, no roads or paths. As he gradually took in the details, Archie could see all the buildings were not exactly identical; they all had subtle differences, and were in various shades of white or cream.

About as big as his home, they were unlike anything Archie had ever seen before. They were all completely spherical in shape, with the lowest parts appearing to be sunk into the ground. Walls and roofs were seamless, but the windows; again round, had been placed in no particular order, and were different in each one, set flush to the walls. From what he could see, the walls were at least a metre thick. He could see no doors at all.

Archie looked over at Hyeke. "What are these places?" he asked her.

"These are the Rearer's homes."

"What are Rearers?"

"I'll explain later." Hyeke promised, looking around her, "Quickly now, we must hurry."

Findley had noticed the low humming noise they had heard inside the canopy was louder now they were outside the protective bubble. It wasn't really intrusive, but gently insistent.

"Where is the noise coming from?" he asked Hyeke.

"I'll show you." She gestured for them to follow her. As they passed the first home, they could see nothing in the windows.

"Where are the people?" asked Archie.

"They are most likely eating at this time." Hyeke glanced over her shoulder at them as she hurried ahead.

In front of them they could see a large circular depression in the ground. As they drew closer they recognised it as similar to an ancient Roman amphitheatre surrounded by tiers of steps leading up to where they stood at the top. The difference was obvious as they started down the clean marble stairs. In the centre, at the bottom, a huge semicircular roof hung like a protective hood over a pair of heavy oak doors; which opened at their approach, and swung silently inward, revealing another flight of stairs.

Hyeke began to walk down the stairs, but stopped and looked back as she realised the boys were not following her. Archie and Findley were standing at the threshold staring down at the floor some twenty feet below.

"The floor is moving!" gasped Findley, forgetting his telepathy.

"This is Ring Eight." Hyeke explained. "It is the outer circle of eight ring roads. They all move, and we can reach the domiciles of all our people from here. Our dwellings are all situated between Ring Eight and Ring Seven."

"What are the others for?" asked Archie, taking his eye protectors off, now that they were out of the blinding light, and following Findley and Hyeke down the stairs.

"They allow us access to the rest of the community." she told him.

"Meal rooms are on Ring Six, near our homes. Gardens and recreation areas, which include drama theatres, libraries; and sports, are all on Ring Five. Primary, Secondary and Tertiary learning are on Ring Four. Hospitals, Reproduction and Life Planning are on Ring Three. Ring Two is Stores and Security, and finally; Ring One and everything inside it is Industry, Maintenance and Control. I will show you. Follow me."

They had reached the bottom of the steps, and the boys watched as the moving road passed by in front of their feet. Hyeke stepped lightly onto the road. The boys watched her, then jumped on, easily balancing on the white rubbery surface as the rolling road picked up speed.

"What about shops?" Archie asked her.

"Shops?" queried Hyeke.

"You know, where you buy stuff."

"I don't understand the concept, buy?" puzzled, Hyeke looked at Archie for an explanation.

"It's when you exchange money for things you want or need."

"Money?" Hyeke's eyebrows went up.

"Money is payment for work. Wow! This is getting complicated." thought Archie.

"I understand. We do not have a commercial system. We learned the lessons of the past dimensions, and our lives are organised very differently."

"What do you mean? How is it possible to live without money?" Archie was shocked.

"Very easy." laughed Hyeke. "I am taking you to Control at the Hub, so you can see how we live for yourselves. Are you hungry?"

"I thought you would never ask!" Findley sighed in relief. "I'm starving!"

"He's always starving!" Archie said, "But not literally, he just likes to eat!"

Hyeke smiled "I know what you mean; I'll take you to a restaurant first."

"How do you get from one ring to another?" asked Findley.

"Intersection shuttles." replied Hyeke. "You'll see for yourselves in a moment. Ah! Here we are." She indicated. The road was slowing down as they came alongside a stationery platform. "Get ready."

The road slowed right down, and they stepped off it and across onto the platform. The road continued on its way.

"We can board a shuttle here." Hyeke led them through a short tunnel, to another platform.

"Wow!" breathed Findley. "It's a rocket! Cool!"

The excited boys gazed admiringly at a shining silver pod nestled in a concave track, close up to the platform.

"It's beautiful!" thought Archie, awed.

The sleek machine, pointed at each end, was two and a half metres high, cylindrical, and as long as a bus. It emitted a low humming sound.

"It is a personal shuttle." Hyeke told them, as she placed her hand inside a small depression on the side. She was rewarded with a green flashing light under her hand.

"What's that?" Archie said.

"It is a security device. Come on."

"Is this your very own shuttle?" Findley asked her as a circular shaped door materialised in the side, and slid silently open.

Hyeke grinned "No. Everybody uses the shuttles whenever they need to."

She stepped inside, the boys following, their eyes greedily taking in every detail. The door slid closed behind them. Luxurious seats were fixed along both sides of the shuttle; and set into the curved roof was a large round illuminated map.

"What's that?" asked Findley, curious.

"That is a map of our Wheel." Hyeke answered him.

"Wheel?" queried Archie

"Wheel Trell. It's the name of our community."

"A Wheel must be the same as a city." Archie sent the thought to Findley.

Hyeke pointed to a place on the outer Ring, where a small green light flashed steadily. "This is where we are now, and here," she moved her finger across to the centre. "Is Control, but we will stop off at the next Ring first, so that we can get something to eat." she added:

"If you sit down, I'll tell the shuttle where we want it to take us."

She smiled at the boys, and they sat down together on the opposite side to the door.

"Wow! These seats are something else, real class." Findley was delighted. He watched, fascinated as the soft, padded cushions wrapped themselves around him, adapted to his shape, and gently firmed up to hold him in place.

"They're brilliant!" Archie thought.

When she was satisfied they were settled, Hyeke made herself comfortable on the seat by the door and said softly, "Ring Six."

The lights on the illuminated map glowed, and began to flash, showing the route Hyeke had requested. "Ready?"

The boys were too excited to answer, and grinning at them Hyeke said "Forward."

Slowly, the shuttle moved. The humming increased slightly but there was no other indication that they were moving at all.

"We must be running on air!" Archie guessed. "What a shame there are no windows."

"Windows would prevent us from going as fast," Hyeke told him.

"Anyway, the speed we are going, you would not be able to see anything. We will be there in a few moments." she leaned back in her seat and closed her eyes.

Archie and Findley watched the movements of the light on the map, indicating the position of the shuttle.

"It's impossible to judge how fast we're going, when we don't know the distance." he thought.

"How far is it?" he asked Hyeke, but there was no response.

"She must have switched off." Findley was following his friend's thinking. The boys sat quietly, thinking over all the extraordinary things that had happened to them since they went to investigate the strange noise at the lodge.

Findley began to feel anxious about the newspapers they had left in the hedge.

"Don't worry, Findley, Craig will find them and guess something is wrong. I'm sure he will deliver them for us." Archie told him, privately thinking that he'd get a terrible row from his older brother when they eventually got back to their own dimension!

"I hope so." Findley was doubtful.

A few minutes later, there was a tiny dinging sound.

"It's like Mum's microwave. We're done!" Archie laughed.

The shuttle light was flashing, stationary at an intersection point on the Ring roads. Archie studied the map closely.

"Look, it is like a wheel, Fin, with other wheels within it, all connected by the spokes."

"Or a huge spider's web." agreed Findley. "Archie, don't you find it odd she's being so nice to us? I mean, we could be invaders or anybody."

"Oh don't be such a wally, Findley. Hyeke, wake up." Archie reached forward and touched her sleeve. She opened her eyes instantly.

"Good, we're here. Come on."

"How do we know we are in the right place? There are no name signs anywhere." wondered Archie.

Hyeke looked at him astonished. She was annoyed with Archie for questioning the fallibility of the system. She told him fiercely, "The shuttle never gets it wrong!"

She marched off through the tunnel, making the boys hurry to keep up.

"You've done it now, Arch." Findley warned him. They caught up with Hyeke as she was stepping onto another rolling road.

Archie hastened to explain. "It's just that things often go wrong in our time, and we have to be prepared for it. I'm sorry to have doubted your system."

Hyeke was mollified. "It doesn't matter. We are more advanced here; I suppose it must be difficult to live in your dimension."

Archie grabbed Findley's arm and they hopped onto the road behind her.

"Sorry." Archie said again.

"Never mind. We'll stop at the next platform. We can eat there." she replied.

This time the boys were ready when the road slowed down, and they stepped off together as if they had been doing it all their lives.

They travelled along to another small tunnel, and as they came out, they were confronted by the most fantastic sight. They were facing a large, open floored cocoon shaped room. They looked up and could see the ceiling was studded with windows, and bright lights. The curved surrounding walls on one side held banks upon banks of rows of engraved pictures.

"Wow, Arch. This is some place." Findley was amazed.

Hyeke took them across to the other side of room and as they stood in front of the pictures, they realised that each one represented a portion of food or drink.

"This is the maitre d'. You can choose whatever you want to eat or drink, but I will have to do the ordering for you, because the machine will not recognise your fingerprints." Hyeke explained.

"It recognises fingerprints?" Archie asked incredulous.

"Naturally, everybody's fingerprints are in the maitre d's data bank. If somebody needs a special diet, or is allergic to a certain kind of food, it is important that the maitre d' is able to prevent them from accidentally ordering the wrong items."

"Can it control how much we eat?" asked Findley, who was definitely on the fat side.

"Oh yes!" answered Hyeke with a smile. "We used to have a great problem with obesity, but since all the maitre d's have been programmed with everyone's details, they can refuse food to anyone who has eaten elsewhere. It has been a great success.

After a lengthy time spent perusing the vast menu, chopping and changing their minds, to Hyeke's private amusement the boys both eventually chose to keep safe and selected sausages, egg, chips and beans, with a glass of water. She obligingly programmed their order, removing a steel numbered disc for each one and included an order of green tea and crackers for herself.

"How does the machine know you are not being greedy?" asked Findley, intrigued.

"When I was sent to collect you from the canopy, special dispensations were granted to me to ensure your well being." She smiled at him, as they walked across together to a large kiosk.

"Oh. I see." Findley was a little confused. He wondered how many people had known about their arrival, and why their well being was so important.

"Don't worry about it now." Archie told him.

Hyeke showed the boys how to insert the discs and wait for a table number to come back. Their number was sixteen.

Quite bewildered now, and wondering when they would actually get to eat their meals, the boys followed Hyeke out of the room, and round a corner, where the boys were confronted by another shimmering curtain.

Chapter Three

Dinner and a History Lesson

"Is that another biohazard curtain?" asked Archie, as they passed through it.

"It has a similar purpose to the canopy, yes, but it is slightly different in that it is comprised of special light-rays. Here we are."

As they stopped at a table bearing the number sixteen, Archie took a quick look at the other occupants of the restaurant. They seemed intent upon their food, almost as if; Archie thought to himself, they had all been warned not to stare at the visitors. He tried smiling at the people at the nearest table, but they ignored him completely.

Uncomfortable, Archie turned back to Hyeke. The table they were standing at seemed to be made of stainless steel, with three stools underneath. The central column of the table was over half a metre in diameter.

Hyeke showed them where to insert their discs into a slot at each place, and in front of the amazed boys. The high-backed stools slid out. When they were seated, the centre top slid back, under the surface of the table top, and a round tray, bearing hot wet towels appeared.

"Hey!" said Archie. "What a fantastic idea!"

They each took a towel and cleaned their hands. When done, the towels were placed back on the tray, which promptly revolved once and disappeared back into the central column.

Next, in rapid succession, all three orders, together with the drinks, cutlery, and napkins were served up through the central column, which then closed itself.

"Wow! This is amazing. I wish we had a table like this at home." thought Archie, picking up his cutlery.

"What about salt and pepper?" demanded Findley.

"Your food is already prepared to your exact taste." admonished Hyeke. "You do not need extra condiments."

Archie looked around at the room. The curved walls gleamed with subdued lighting, softly reflected in the stainless steel tables and high backed stools. Although he was in a fairly familiar environment, he felt something was different, strange even. He studied the other diners for a minute. They all seemed to be enjoying their food, laughing and smiling as they ate, occasionally nodding their heads and interacting normally.

Noise! Archie thought to himself. Because the people here communicated by thought transference, there was little sound at all, apart from the muted sounds of cutlery on plates. It was so quiet here.

He remembered the loud hubbub of the service stations his father took him to eat at when he stayed with him, and he realised, for the first time, how much nicer it was to be able to eat without the sounds of people arguing and over-tired children screaming in the background.

There must be at least seventy tables occupied, that he could see. He knew this was the first place they had seen any other people, but he was becoming a little uneasy. He wanted to ask Findley if he had noticed, but he was worried that Hyeke would pick up his thoughts and be offended. He decided to wait until he could talk to him privately, and began to eat.

Although it was a very ordinary meal, the food was perfectly cooked, and he knew for sure it was the best he had ever tasted.

When they had finished eating, Hyeke took the disc from the table, and the central column opened up and the plates slid down the incline back to the centre again. As they watched them disappear, their chairs slid out and a long, thin wand came up, and waved around the entire surface of the table.

"What is that for?" asked Findley.

"That is only a steam wand. It is cleaning the table for the next diners. Now, if you are ready I'll take you to the rest room."

The boys exchanged embarrassed glances. So Findley had noticed, Archie thought to himself.

Seeing their hesitation, Hyeke laughed "Come on, I promise not to watch!"

Feeling rather foolish, they shuffled along behind as Hyeke led the way out of the dining room through a small passage leading to an annexe. As they approached, the door opened automatically, and closed behind them. Archie and Findley gazed around them in surprise. The gleaming pale blue floors, walls and ceilings seemed seamless, curving into each other with no corners. They could see no toilet cubicles, or washing facilities in the room. Archie thought perhaps they had misunderstood what Hyeke meant by restroom. He noticed doors set flush into the walls; they were set about two metres apart either side along the length of the long, narrow room. There were large picture panels above each door, some were red, and some green.

"The red panel means it is occupied." thought Archie

"Yes" agreed Findley, "but how do we get in?"

"Just push a door with a green picture above," said Hyeke. "I will meet you out here when you are ready."

Archie went to push an unoccupied door and it opened before he reached it. "No physical contact. That's neat!" thought Archie, as he went in.

Findley, seeing Archie was getting on all right, copied him and went in the room next door.

"Archie?" Findley's thoughts were clearly heard by Archie "Where are all the boys?"

"I don't know Fin, but they must be in another part of the Wheel, I suppose. Hey! This room is cool. What is yours like?"

"Same as yours, I'd guess. There is everything in here that anyone would ever need. Have you seen the toilet? I nearly didn't recognise it!"

There was silence as the boys finished their ablutions. You could never catch any germs or anything nasty in here Archie noted, as his every move was pre-empted. When he sat on the toilet he was suspended on a cushion of warm air, which, when he finished changed to a wash of warm water, followed by a drying warm air, everything being quickly siphoned away.

His hands were washed and dried after he placed them in a small aperture in the wall, without any effort on his part at all, though he noticed the rainbow mixture was still shimmering on his skin, even after washing.

As he made his way toward the door, he recognised a slim, cylindrical shower cubicle, and saw strange apertures on the wall. One had a picture he thought resembled a laundry basket, and Arch wondered if his dusty jeans would get washed if he put them inside. He decided not to try it out this time. He could think of nothing more embarrassing if he didn't get them back!

The door opened silently to let him out, and he marvelled again at how hygienic everything was. From entry to exit, he had not had to touch anything in the room.

As he watched Findley emerge from his cubicle, looking rather red in the face, Archie guessed he'd been looking at the female paraphernalia he'd seen in his own cubicle.

He grinned at his friend, and looked round for Hyeke. She was standing at the entrance to the long room, and appeared to be communicating with an older woman. Archie could see something seemed to be worrying her. She looked round and saw the boys. Her face changed quickly and she smiled as they approached her.

"Ready?" she asked. They nodded, and she shepherded them through the now open door, past the woman, who smiled at them as they went by.

"We're going to the Control room now."

The boys were getting to know the routine; and obediently followed Hyeke back through the dining room and out through the barrier curtain and through the tunnel taking them to the rolling road. A short trip took them to the next intersection, and they settled themselves comfortably in the seats of another identical shuttle.

This time, the trip was rather longer. Archie thought how wonderful it would be if he could travel as easily in his own home town. No cars or vehicles would mean an end to pollution, road rage or traffic jams. He was about to ask Hyeke how they transported supplies, but then remembered her habit of switching off when travelling on shuttles. He wondered if she could sleep at will anywhere, and decided she probably could.

Findley's thoughts interrupted his musings. "You know Arch," he began.

"I've been thinking. There must be boys and men about somewhere. We'll most likely see them at the Control Centre."

"Yes." agreed Archie. "We'll find out soon enough."

As they watched the flashing shuttle light draw closer to the control centre, they were both excited and a little apprehensive. They exchanged nervous grins as the shuttle stopped and they heard the familiar ting announce their arrival.

Hyeke woke up and commanded the door to open. Released from their seats, the boys disembarked and followed her out onto the platform. They could see immediately this was very different from anything they had seen before. Instead of the usual small tunnel, there were huge banks of stairs, leading off in different directions

A woman, aged about thirty, was waiting for them. Her long blonde hair, hung loosely down her back, but was drawn back off her face with scarlet clips. She was dressed in a smart scarlet and gold tunic, which had epaulettes on the shoulders, and she looked very efficient and important.

She greeted Hyeke with a nod and they exchanged thoughts the boys could not follow. Hyeke smiled and turned to the boys.

"This is Starmol. She is the Controller this week. She is going to show you around and explain some things I know have been puzzling you." she turned to step back into the shuttle.

"You're not leaving us?" Findley blurted out, forgetting in his panic to send the question as a thought. "How will we get back? We can't find our way on our own!"

Hyeke stopped and turned to him. "I have to leave you but I promise it will only be for a short time. There is nothing at all for you to be concerned about. I will be back later. There is a small matter I must attend to. Meantime Starmol will take good care of you. Go with her. Goodbye for now, there is much for you to learn." she turned away and stepped aboard the shuttle.

As the door closed behind her, the boys looked at each other in dismay. Before they could think further, they heard Starmol's voice in their heads; it sounded calm and more measured than Hyeke's younger, lighter voice. The boys instinctively relaxed.

"Hyeke tells me you are from the third dimension. It is very good that you are here, but I know our lives must seem to be very different from yours. I will take you to the Hub first I think. It will help you to understand us a little better."

Starmol led the boys across a wide expanse of marble to a flight of stairs with a small platform at the foot. She turned and smiled at them.

"Step onto the platform and stand still." When the boys were huddled together with her, she spoke aloud "Up. To the top floor. Hold the safety rail please."

The auto stairs took on a life of their own, and whizzed them all, first to one landing and then another.

"Wow!" thought Findley "This is some cool escalator Arch!" They heard Starmol laugh out loud. "I agree Findley, I never tire of it!"

Findley shuffled his feet, embarrassed his thoughts had been overheard.

They had arrived at the entrance to a large office like room, and they stepped off the platform, Starmol shepherding them forward, and offering them seats.

As he sat down Archie was busy looking around. "I've noticed all your buildings are about two thirds above ground, but they are all accessed by stairs underneath. There are many windows, but why are there no doors on the outside?"

Starmol was taken aback. "Outside doors? We do not need them. Nobody ever goes outside except the riders and the farmers unless there is an emergency, such as when Hyeke came to fetch you from the canopy."

"Why?" asked Findley "The weather was absolutely brilliant. We noticed how warm and bright it was out there."

"Yes." agreed Starmol, "but the canopy was protecting you."

"Protecting us from what?" asked Archie "That rat?"

"Rat? Oh the raptorvor. Among other things, yes, but mostly it was protecting you from a sudden change in the weather," explained Starmol. "We have learned many things in our fight for survival, but we have no power over the climate yet. Our planet is still recovering from the ravages wrought by men from other dimensions. We are doing all we can, but it will be many more millennia before the ecological balance is fully restored."

"Is that why your windows are so thick and brown?" Archie asked her.

"Yes, partly to prevent the fierce storms from breaking them, but also to protect us from the harmful rays of the sun, while still allowing us to enjoy the natural light, which we value very much. In your Dimension, such precautions were not necessary. There was a layer of ozone in the atmosphere above Earth, which acted as a natural shield."

Starmol shrugged her shoulders.

"So much damage was done through ignorance and man's greed. At the end of your dimension our planet was dying from pollution. Many millions of people choked to death because they could not breathe the poisoned air. Fresh water became very scarce.

There were huge arguments between the countries. Some people realised what was happening, others simply did not care. Some tried to stop the waste of the planets natural resources like oil and coal, but they were overruled by the greed of others."

"What happened?" asked Findley.

"As far as we can find out from our archives, powerful countries bombed weaker ones to take control of their oil and fresh water. That just meant they were used up even faster; almost all the rain forests were felled, before man came to his senses and realised a large part of the oxygen we need to breathe came from the trees."

"I learned about the rainforests in school. They're in Brazil, they've cleared a lot of it to rear cattle for our beef-burgers." Findley thought.

"I think they realised what damage they were doing and stopped. Didn't they?" Archie was confused.

"We have certainly learned there were huge misinformation schemes, and the public were rarely told the truth." Starmol agreed.

"People felt betrayed by their leaders and so they turned to the different religious orders for guidance and comfort. This led expansionist religions into huge religious wars. None had any time for any of the others, all believing their way was the only way."

"What is this place Starmol?" Findley asked her, privately feeling thoroughly bored with the history lesson.

"This is the part of the Hub that deals with our past, Findley. It holds all our archives. All our progress is documented here too." she told him. "Come over here with me."

Archie, even more disinterested than Findley, hung back as Starmol led them to a circular alcove. He noticed several small tunnels in the walls, and he thought he'd just take a quick look.

Glancing quickly at Starmol, he could see she was occupied, placing some sort of apparatus on Findley's head. Arch winked quickly at his friend and darted into the nearest tunnel before she noticed.

As he entered the dark tunnel, Archie was terrified to feel his feet suddenly leave the ground, and his body began to spin, he thought he might be sick, or even black out. He span faster and faster, until he actually felt himself bouncing hard against the walls; then he found he was standing on absolutely nothing, with just the pressure of the air around him holding his body up and preventing him from falling.

Descending in a sudden rush, his feet hit the floor fast, and he sat down hard on his bottom with a heavy thump.

The first thing he was aware of was the noise. He could see he was in a large room. It had great big windows along one side. He was sitting on a thickly piled carpet, for which he was very grateful. The fall had been quite uncomfortable. Directly in front of him was a huge antique desk. Peering carefully around the side of the desk Archie could see about twenty people, all men, seated at a long conference table not far away from him, drinking coffee. They all seemed to be talking at once, until the man positioned at the top rapped the table with a gavel. Everyone fell silent as he said.

"I have called you all to this meeting in order to discuss the new contracts to provide storage containers filled with drinking water for the Government's Survival Project." He laughed nastily.

"We all know these places are never going to be used, just as all those A bomb shelters built in the last millennium never were either. It's a waste of money in my opinion. However, we shall keep to the specifications required in the contract. As usual, and most advantageously to us, they are vague in the extreme; two thousand cubic meters of tap water to be stored in sealed containers, housed in supporting cages per survival facility..."

Archie stopped listening. He looked hard at the men. Their skins were all colours, ranging from Chinese to dark brown. They all seemed quite fat, and well dressed, in long, colourful tunics. As his eyes travelled downwards, taking in the exquisite embroideries on their unusual clothes, he noticed the men's feet. He was surprised to see none of them were wearing shoes. Instead of any footwear it appeared as if they had dipped their feet in a thick plastic. He could see no sign of any of the men wearing socks, he could even see the men's toes, and their toenails were all evenly cut and well manicured. Some were even wearing nail varnish on them!

How strange! It must be some kind of fashion, he thought, in amusement. What on earth is this place? Where have I landed up now? he wondered, bemused.

The loud voices eventually penetrated his amusement. He listened, not liking what he heard. They seemed to be arguing about doing something illegal; and he shrank back, scared they would discover him; he knew the men would not be pleased if they found him.

He could smell coffee, and looking behind him, he nearly jumped out of his skin with fright. A small round robot was watching him, holding out a mug of coffee. He crept right underneath the desk out of sight. To Archie's horror, the machine tried to follow him.

"I don't want any!" he hissed. The robot spoke "Coffee, black, white, sugar, cream?"

Archie was desperate "No!" he said. He looked over at the men, they hadn't heard him, and thankfully the robot had taken the hint and moved to the side of the desk.

The men were getting angry. Archie understood most of the men wanted to use more expensive materials for the water stores, while the man in charge was arguing about costs.

It was very hot under the desk and Archie wished the men would go, so he could find out where he was.

The man who was leading the argument for better materials, suddenly stood up.

"I will not be a party to using this inferior material," he shouted, "We already know it absorbs chemicals stored close to it. The water will be so contaminated by the time it is needed, it will be undrinkable. We should be thinking about using reinforced glass, which could be protected on the outside by a thick plastic coating. The glass will be a complete barrier to the chemicals in the plastic, and prevent any leaching into the water. I cannot countenance using anything else."

He walked out of the room, and slammed the door behind him.

The man with the gavel sneered, "Bill worries too much. Nobody is ever going to actually live in these Survival Systems. So, are we all agreed?"

Archie, sickened, watched as they all used their votes to use the cheap plastic. He was uncomfortable, and cramped under the desk. He stretched his legs without thinking. There was a crash as his feet pushed the coffee robot over. Cups saucers, and streams of coffee, sugar and cream fell out of the various slots of the machine, and it bleated over and over again... "Coffee, black coffee, white coffee..."

"What the hell?" the men jumped to their feet and ran over to the desk. Archie made himself as small as he could. One man looked under the desk. "Hey! What do we have here? I do believe it's a nasty little spy!"

Chapter Four

How the world nearly ended

The man reached for Archie, and grabbing him hard by the arm, he roughly pulled the boy out from under the desk, and onto his feet.

"What were you doing, hiding under there? How did you get in?" he thundered.

Poor Archie stammered "W...w...which year is this?"

The man roared "What do you mean, which year? This is 2250 as well you know my boy. Now answer my question! What are you doing here? Who sent you?" he took Archie by his arms and began to shake him hard. Archie's head began to spin, and everything went black.

The next thing he knew, he was lying flat on the floor at the Control Centre, being shaken gently, as Findley, his face crinkled with worry, asked him what had happened.

"We were all so scared Archie. They thought you had got lost. I had to tell them I saw you go into the tunnel. Starmol told me those tunnels are memory holes, nobody is allowed to go into them alone. They are for training the Controllers. Are you okay Archie? Where did you go?" He was so scared for Archie, Findley had forgotten to use telepathy.

Archie took a long drink from the glass of water the boy was holding, and climbed unsteadily to his feet, and shook his head. "It was dead weird, Findley. I was like... flown backwards to 2250."

"2250 What's that?"

"The year 2250! I was stuck in a room, hiding from a crowd of men. Findley, I heard them agreeing to use cheap plastic for the drinking water stores in the survival pods!"

"What?" Findley did not understand.

Starmol came bustling up to the boys. "Oh good! You are awake! How do you feel?" she lifted Archie's chin and looked into his eyes. "You seem to have recovered very quickly. It is a good thing you did not choose one of the war memory tunnels, you could have been injured! Now I think you should learn about things the easy way Archie, with your friend."

Archie shrugged, and grimaced at Findley. "It looks like we do not have any choice! Will it take long?" he asked as Starmol gently placed the light see through apparatus over their heads.

"No, this is just to give you some idea. These will allow you to hear what is happening and follow what is on the screens. Just relax and you will see for yourselves; what happened to our planet, and how we came to survive. We will start with your Dimension first."

She spoke rapidly, giving instructions to the screen. As they watched, the walls and the ceiling of the alcove shivered and changed, becoming a giant screen surrounding them both. The boys found themselves seated at the rear of a huge room, where hundreds of men and woman were seated at tiers of desks. All had microphones before them and each wore interpreting headsets. A woman sat on Archie's right.

"What is happening? Archie asked her.

"Do you not know? This is the World Forum, "she told them. "Leaders from all the countries in the world have been invited to be involved in the decision process. Why are you here?"

Archie quickly introduced himself and explained that he and Findley were on a fact finding mission from school, then asked her,

"What decision process?"

"Hush. That is the leader of the most powerful country in the world. He's getting ready to speak."

"Is he the American president?"

"No." replied the woman. America and Japan agreed to join together with China about two hundred years ago. They called themselves the United States of Chipanica. It was China's idea to start with. They planned well, starting at the end of the first millennium."

"How could they do that?" Findley scoffed.

"They had few natural resources, but some very clever scientists, and technologists. They had such a huge population, many, many millions, and they realised that as long as their numbers kept increasing, they would never be able to lift their people out of poverty. They also saw they would never have sufficient resources to compete commercially with the rest of the world. So their leaders decided on drastic action."

"What did they do?" Archie asked.

"They passed a law allowing only one child per family. This had two far reaching consequences."

"So none of the Chinese have any brothers or sisters?" asked Findley appalled.

"That is exactly right, Findley. To begin with they let people try again if the first baby was a girl, but later they kept very strictly to the law." The woman sighed.

"The problem was the girl babies."

"Why?" asked Archie.

"The trouble was, the Chinese preferred boy babies. This meant if they could only have one baby, the parents wanted it to be a boy. So if an unfortunate woman gave birth to a girl, her husband would take it away, and either; drown it in the nearest river, or more often leave it on the doorstep of an orphanage in the middle of the night.

There were always at least two million girl babies in the orphanages at any one time. This would go on until the family had a baby boy."

"What happened to all the girls?" Archie wanted to know.

"They were put up for adoption." The woman told him. "Many desperate couples travelled from all over the world to find a child. Even holiday makers were encouraged by taxi-drivers. If they were found to be childless, they would be driven on a sightseeing tour which included the orphanages, and once they'd seen the babies, some of them found it impossible to say no."

"You said there were two results." Archie wondered as he watched the men on the rostrum arguing angrily. "What was the other one?"

"Well, when eventually the young men grew up, healthy, well nourished and educated to the highest levels their parents could afford, there was just one thing they lacked."

"Girls!" said Findley.

"Exactly," she agreed. "By this time there was only one girl for about every fifteen men."

"So what happened?"

"The men who were unlucky at home searched the internet for Chinese girls. They met, and married, and the husbands joined them in their adopted countries. Because the men were highly educated, and had skills the countries needed, there was usually no trouble with the immigration laws. Once married, they could raise as many children as they wanted. They worked hard, and in time gained full citizenship. But no matter where they lived, or worked, their first loyalty was always to China."

"That makes sense. Clever." agreed Archie.

"Of course, you have to remember this has been a slow process, over the course of two or three hundred years. By the time America, for instance, realised almost a third of their population was Chinese they were thoroughly integrated."

"Yes, I understand. A very long term project indeed."

"Of course China in the meantime, freed from the tremendous burden of feeding an enormous population; has done very well, being able to concentrate on increasing their technology, and now the rest of the world finds itself more and more dependent on them. Most importantly, the Chinese in their adoptive countries; are in many cases being elected to very powerful positions, from which they are able to ensure the peaceful amalgamation of more and more countries, without any fighting, and it has all worked extremely well."

"It's a scary thought, China being in charge." Findley fidgeted, restless.

"It isn't like that. China is not really in charge. Well," she paused. "Chipanican people elected their leaders. Europe attempted to do something similar. They called themselves the European States, but it was not a success. There was a huge amount of corruption, followed by a complete lack of trust. Germany and France seemed to be in charge, and quite a few of the smaller countries refused to join."

"What are those men arguing about?" Archie asked her as the volume of noise reached a crescendo.

"Listen, you can hear for yourselves." The woman leaned forward and took up two tiny coils from the bench in front of them and handed them to the boys.

After fitting the slim wires in their ears they could clearly hear the announcer requesting silence for the British Prime Minister. She began to speak, as Archie and Findley listened.

"The points system is a total nonsense. You must see it defeats the whole principle. We have agreed to consume the least number of points possible and now we have other countries attempting to barter for our unused points to use themselves to support their greedy lifestyle."

"What points system?" Findley wondered.

"All the countries in the contract have been allocated an agreed number of points based on population numbers and usage of fuels." the woman told them, "It started off as a good idea, to help reduce emissions of greenhouse gases that were depleting the protective ozone layer. But the greedy ones quickly latched onto the idea of buying points from the countries that had not used them all."

"Ridiculous." snorted Archie."I remember something on television about it. Several countries would not even agree to cut their emissions at all." They watched as the various leaders continued to argue.

"What are those masks on their faces for?" asked Findley as the scene changed to a later period.

The woman had disappeared, and Starmol joined them in their virtual world. "Extra oxygen, to help with their breathing." explained Starmol. "The air is getting very bad, and still they argue."

"It doesn't make sense," thought Archie.

"No," Starmol agreed.

"So what happened?" asked Findley.

"Nothing was resolved. The countries continued to disagree about how the planet should be protected from pollution. The greedy ones didn't care at all. Refused to believe there was any problem. Eventually, it led to bitterness, sanctions, and at the end, finally outright fighting. There were many wars in different parts of the world. The fighting just added to the planet's troubles, and in time, it grew so bad, some of the country's leaders realised the only way the human race could survive would be if they went underground. So they made survival plans, and built underground pods."

"Survival plans? You mean bunkers?" asked Findley.

"Not just bunkers. They were far more sophisticated than that. They built huge under-ground towns, using tunnels in the mountains, and large caverns, old mines, anything that could be completely cut off and self contained. I'll take you Down to see one later, if you would like."

"What about food and water, and how could they breathe?" asked Archie.

"They had underground farms, growing crops, fruit and vegetables. Huge eco-systems supplied air. They also had vast libraries, records. Everything you can think of. They even had animals. No expense was spared to save the leaders and their families, doctors, the clever scientists and technicians."

"So they were prepared for anything."

"Almost anything, yes. Meanwhile the ordinary people turned to religion for guidance, but the various factions could not agree, and eventually the fighting developed into outright atomic war. The entire planet's equilibrium was unbalanced, and in the end it sort of fought back."

"How could it do that?" Findley wanted to know.

"Long dead volcanoes were rocked back to life by the many atomic explosions, and many new ones were created, spewing up lava and gases all over the surface of the planet. Earthquakes rocked the continents."

Starmol leaned forward and said "Fourth Dimension" to the screen. The boys watched fascinated as the screen showed the violence of the weather storms, and earthquakes shaking the planet. Gradually as they watched, the screen showed ash flying about, thicker and thicker until the entire screen was dark.

"What's happening?" asked Findley.

"When the earthquakes stopped and the volcanoes quietened, there was a thick layer of ash in the earth's atmosphere. It blotted out the sun, and gradually everywhere grew extremely cold."

"Another ice-age," mused Archie.

"Yes," Starmol agreed. "But we call it the ice-over. It lasted two dimensions."

"So where is Britain?" Archie wanted to know.

Starmol answered him. "Lost, Archie, like all the other countries. When the ice-over melted, the land was divided by water into four roughly equal parts."

"Which part are we in?" demanded Archie.

"Artross." Starmol answered, "The other three are Clunn, Preeda and Zero."

"Strange names." thought Findley.

"They are all named after the leaders of the different groups of survivors," explained

Starmol. "All except Zero, we haven't found any survivors there."

"Wow! So what happened to all the people and animals?" asked Findley.

"A small number survived underground. Almost all perished of course, and it took

thousands of years for the radiation to degrade sufficiently to a level safe enough for life to resume outside."

"What about the air?" Archie asked.

"Without the intervention of man, trees grew again, and the forests regenerated themselves. These gave food and shelter for insects, birds and animals, and the ecological balance of the planet is beginning to be restored. It has taken many dimensions," she added, "to reach this stage. We still suffer from dreadful storms and winds. This is why our houses are round. It is the best shape to withstand the hurricanes."

"What sort of power do you have? To use for cooking and heating for instance; and running machinery?" Archie queried.

"We use the sun, naturally!" Starmol was astonished at the question. "What else is there?"

"Electricity?" ventured Archie.

"Never heard of it!" said Starmol. "Everything we use is powered by the sun. The walls of our homes absorb the heat and evenly distribute it."

"Doesn't it get too hot?" Archie asked.

"No. We use heat exchangers, the heat is stored and released when needed."

"What about atomic energy?" Findley wondered.

"Don't you think atomic energy has been the cause of enough damage already? We would be fools indeed if we couldn't learn a lesson as big as that from our predecessors. We wouldn't deserve to survive." Starmol shuddered.

"What about cold?" Archie wanted to know.

"The climate of Artross is very temperate; hardly ever gets very cold. When it does,

we go 'Down'."

"Down?"

"Underground." answered Starmol.

"How many people live here in Wheel Trell?" Archie asked her.

"We have three hundred and forty adults, and three tiers of children in Wheel Trell."

"What do you mean? Tiers?"

"I see I must explain," Starmol nodded. "Originally, there were only twenty-eight of my ancestors left when they came up to the surface, several hundred years ago now. To begin with, they concentrated on making the living-quarters safe, and increasing their numbers. Gradually, they evolved the system we have today.

All the Wheels on Artross were populated by those original twenty-eight. Some Wheels started to increase too rapidly, and they had difficulty feeding every-one, so we now have a system of tiers. Every five years, our technicians start the process of incubating eight babies. They are not always successful, but we only begin another set if they all fail. This way, we are able to control our population."

"What happens if the earthquakes are bad? Is there room 'Down' for everybody?" Findley was anxious to know.

"Every Wheel now has their own 'Down'. It makes things much easier. They can escape from the weather very quickly, and if a Wheel is destroyed, our civilisation will still survive."

"How long can you stay 'Down'?" Archie wondered.

"We can stay 'Down' for as long as necessary." Starmol answered.

"Our people lived underground for many thousands of years. The air outside wasn't safe to breathe, so they couldn't live on the surface. They built huge underground complexes, something like our Wheel, but hundreds of metres deep."

"What did they eat?"

"They had everything they needed to grow and process food. Remember, after the wars and during the ice-over, only a few people were left. They had to adapt very quickly.

They passed down their knowledge and were always discovering newer and better survival methods. Their descendants through the hundreds of years underground gradually learned better ways to survive in their enforced incarceration.

Hundreds of generations of people never saw daylight, but they all knew that one day their great, great, great grand children would get back to the surface. They grew their own food, reared sheep and even had pets. They had very carefully engineered ecological systems. They had to be completely self-sufficient. If not, they died, and many did. It's as simple as that." Starmol shrugged.

"How do you know all this?" Archie asked.

"From the records the survivors kept in their archives. Very occasionally another pod is discovered, but we have only ever found one with live people in it. There were just six left. The rest had succumbed to a lack of hope, and had forgotten how to survive. We found them just in time. Look," she turned to the screen.

"'Down'" she said. The screen obediently showed a large cavern, and Starmol guided the cameras, so the boys could see inside. "See," she said, "That's where we found the last survivors."

Archie and Findley watched as they were taken via the virtual cameras through the many tunnels of living quarters of people who had for centuries lived underground. Lights hung from the high ceilings, and there were green plants everywhere.

There were huge areas of space, for recreation, small dormitories off the side tunnels for individual families. Banks of technological equipment covered the walls. There were also many large murals, beautiful works of art adorning some of the walls. Starmol told the fascinated boys,

"This is where my ancestors lived, hundreds of years ago. As I told you, 'Down' is still an operational town, and when the earthquakes are bad, we return here for safety."

The camera was now showing miles of terraced walls that seemed to be planted with crops.

"Wow! The whole place looks so organised, I don't know, it reminds me a bit of a giant anthill." Archie said.

He leaned forward, "Look, there's a river." he looked round at Starmol. "Perhaps they used the power of the water to run their systems?"

"That's quite right, Archie. They were lucky to have a deep underground river, that was so deep it was uncontaminated by what was happening on the earth's surface.

We still use the power of the water to this day, and it is still the freshest and cleanest we can find."

"Is the water up on the surface still contaminated then?" asked Findley, worried about the water that was served with their meal.

"No, the whole of Artross is completely clear of any contamination. It is only the uncertain weather we have to contend with now." Starmol leaned forward,

"Off." She commanded and the screen obediently went blank.

"That's enough history for now. Would you like to go 'Down' and see it for real?

"Wow! Yes, please!" they both answered in unison.

"Fine." Starmol stood up and went over to the stairs. "Stand here!" she indicated, wrapping her arms around the shoulders of the two boys.

She said "Down." The stairs moved, slowly at first, then gathered speed as the boys reached out and held the safety rails tightly.

Chapter Five

'Down' under Artross

A few moments later, they arrived back at the platform. Starmol waved a hand towards the wall, and a small door opened for them. They stepped inside and saw they were at the end of a long narrow tunnel. There were poles, about half a metre apart, fixed into the white rubbery surface which sloped downwards.

"It's another rolling road!" thought Archie.

"No, this is only a path leading to another road. It gets quite fast, so hold onto the poles," Starmol told them.

The road gathered speed quickly and soon the boys were hanging on for dear life. The humming sound they associated with the other roads was very loud here, and Findley thought it was a good thing they did not have to shout to be heard.

Archie agreed, "This is some ride! I suppose it has to go fast when you are evacuating all the people? Is this the only way 'Down'?" he asked.

Starmol shook her head. "No, Archie, there are many ways 'Down', as many as twenty, I think."

"Why are there so many?" Findley wanted to know.

"That would be so you couldn't be trapped down there, if one of the tunnels collapsed in an earthquake. Is that right Starmol?"

"Yes." she agreed.

The path in the tunnel was slowing down and the boys blinked as they came out into a huge white cavern. All around the sides were entrances to tunnels exactly like the one the boys had arrived here from.

"It's awesome!" breathed Findley.

"Massive!" Archie nodded. "Where is the way into the town?"

"Oh we haven't arrived there yet. We are only five thousand feet down." The boys followed her as she pointed towards the centre. There they could see a large, round steel capsule.

"It looks like a gas-o-meter!" said Findley.

"It may look like that in structure, yes, but it is actually a giant elevator!" Starmol laughed.

As they approached the doors, they obligingly opened and the boys, eyes large with excitement, stepped inside.

Starmol directed them to lie on two of the many couches, which were fixed to the floor. She made sure the straps were fastened tightly across them.

"You may as well have a little nap," she suggested, "It takes nearly an hour to reach

'Down.' Hold onto your stomachs!" Starmol lay on the couch next to Archie, buckled her belt and said softly "'Down.'"

The elevator dropped with sickening speed, and Findley was suddenly very scared.

"It's okay mate, just pretend you are a miner, going down in the lift to dig for gold!" Archie's voice comforted Findley, and he felt better.

"This is some adventure, Archie. The kids at school will never believe us!"

"I know," Archie agreed, "I keep thinking I must be dreaming!"

The boys were too excited to sleep, their heads were buzzing with questions, but Starmol had taken her own advice and was sound asleep.

Archie looked at his watch, but discovered with dismay it had stopped at seven o'clock. He shook it hard, but the second hand refused to move. He leaned over and reached across and touched his friend's arm.

"Findley, what time is it?"

"It's just on seven o'clock." he murmured, half asleep.

"It can't be, Findley. That was when we stepped into the future funnel. Mine stopped then too. Maybe batteries don't work in this dimension. That would explain why our mobiles are dead too."

"Probably." Findley grinned, "As long as they keep feeding us, it doesn't matter, does it!"

There was a slight jolt, and the boys noticed the elevator had stopped, and Starmol was getting up. They quickly unfastened their belts and stood up, anxious to see where they were.

As they walked out of the elevator, the first thing they noticed was how warm it was.

"It must be because we are deep underground." Archie thought.

Starmol nodded at him as she led the way to a large opening in the wall, the boys stepped through, and they were stunned to find they were standing in a large open space.

"Except for the roof, way up there, we could be in a field," thought Archie.

"This is the exercise area for the animals. The sheep graze here, when there is no hay, but since we have lived in Artross, we have been able to keep them well supplied."

"Are there still sheep living down here?" Archie asked.

"Oh yes, look over there," she pointed and they could see several sheep gathered at the gate on the other side of the area.

"They are being fed now." They walked over to the sheep, which took no notice of the newcomers, concentrating on eating.

"Just like ours!" Findley said wondering.

"Not quite the same, said Starmol. These look the same as yours, but they are bred for wool, and they shed their fleece twice a year.

"Shed? Don't you have to shear them? Wow! our farmers would love sheep like that, and to get two fleeces a year. Ours are only sheared once." he added.

"Yes, but we have had many years in which to concentrate on breeding the type of animals we need. There are other sheep, which are in a different field, and they have no fleece at all. They are bred purely for our meat." she told them.

"Are they down here too?" asked Findley. "It seems a bit cruel to me."

"Not at all. They have always lived 'Down' and know no other way of life. When our ancestors reached the surface, they had all sorts of difficulties, and they had to breed new varieties of sheep, which could deal with the fluctuating temperatures, insects and the like. We have no problems with the animals down here, because they are used to it."

"Would you like to see the kitchens?" she smiled at Findley, who nodded enthusiastically.

They entered a small doorway which led through a short tunnel to a large room. A woman was directing a steam wand around the work surfaces, and she stopped as she noticed the trio at the door.

"Another 'quake?" she asked them.

"No, said Starmol. "Boys, let me introduce Jamessa. These are our visitors, Archie and Findley, they arrived this morning and Findley is very interested in our food" she smiled.

"That's good, you like cooking, do you?" she asked Findley.

"I think he prefers eating!" Archie laughed.

"He is someone after my own heart!" she patted her ample body, and said "Where do you think all this came from?" Findley grinned, he liked Jamessa already; being quite fat himself, it was nice to find somebody else who approved of eating.

Jamessa bustled about, finding a plate of buns and drinks for the boys. They sat at a large old wooden table and tucked in.

Starmol and Jamessa walked over to the door, communicating silently while the boys enjoyed their buns, and when they were finished, Starmol said she would show the boys the domestic quarters.

As they walked along, Starmol explained that there were still some people living 'Down', as it was necessary to keep the underground town functioning normally.

"One day we hope it will be like a museum, which our great, great grand children will be able to visit to find out how our ancestors lived, but it must be kept in a state of readiness, for now because the weather is still too unpredictable, and the earthquakes too frequent."

"Have you had to come 'Down' because of an earthquake?" Archie asked her.

"Yes," she answered, "We have had to evacuate Artross three times in my life, so far. Fortunately, not for too long each time. I think the longest time was for two weeks."

"Two whole weeks?" Archie was shocked.

"Yes, our storms can rage for a long time you know, and although our buildings are made to withstand them, it is a lot safer down here."

They were approaching a wide tunnel, which had doors on either side.

"These are the private homes of the people who care for the town, but Jamessa told me you could see her place. Here we are."

She opened a door and they stepped inside a small hall, which they went through into a medium sized room. There were bookcases, and pictures. A comfortable easy chair was placed in a corner On one wall was a mural, and as the fascinated boys watched it, the scene, depicting the sea, showed boats and ships moving across the water.

"Wow. That's neat!" Findley loved the sea, and decided, the mural was one of the best things he had seen here so far, apart from the maitre d'.

Archie grinned at him "Trust you to put food first!" he thought, as they were shown the bedroom, which was a small room with lots of green plants hanging over the small neatly made bed.

"How fresh it is in here!" he thought, and tried the mattress with his fingers. "It is so soft!" he said. "What is the mattress made of?"

"Sheep's wool, Starmol replied, "there are no man-made fibres in this room, that it is why everywhere smells so fresh."

"Where is the kitchen?" asked Findley as Starmol showed them out, "and the bathroom?"

"Everyone eats at the meal rooms, and they use the restrooms, just as we do in Artross. It saves space, and water.

There is not much more to see that would interest you, apart from the archives. Just through here." She directed them into another huge area, but this time every centimetre of space on all the walls, was covered with writing.

"What is this place? Are those names?" he asked as he studied the wall. There are many different languages here, but most of it seems to be in Latin."

"Yes, for most of the time, my ancestors conversed in Latin. Remember the majority of original survivors were scientists and technologists, educated men and women, from widely different backgrounds, and in order to communicate easily, they used Latin. That was before they learned thought transference, of course. After that they could communicate in any language and always be understood."

"How could that work?" asked Archie.

"I cannot say, I only know it does," said Starmol. "Now, I think we should be making our way back."

"What happened to all these people?" asked Findley. "I mean, where are the bodies?"

Starmol was startled by the question.

"The bodies of the people who died here were incinerated.

I know in many countries in your dimension, they are buried in the ground, but there was no room for them to be able to do that here, so they were burned and the ashes returned to the underground fields, and along the wall terraces, where we still grow crops to this day, just in case they are needed.

As you see," she pointed to the wall, "records of their names, and the year of their death were all kept here. There has been an attempt made to collate them all to add to our libraries in Artross. Several historians are working on the project to this day, but it will be some time before the work is finished."

Starmol ushered the boys back to the elevator, and strapped them to the couches as before.

As the elevator sped upwards, Archie reflected on how life must have been, living down there, for hundreds of generations.

He was not at all sure that he would be happy to live like that, and he could understand why some of the survival pods had been discovered empty. It must be difficult to keep hoping for so long. He thought the will to live must have been especially strong in those groups that had made it to the outside. He knew there must have been times when the people disagreed, even fought, over small insignificant things, and was privately amazed that any had survived at all.

It just goes to show, he thought, as he dozed off.

It seemed only a few seconds later, Starmol was busy unbuckling the restraining belts on his couch. "We're back, Archie, did you sleep well?" she smiled at the boy, as he shook himself and climbed off his seat.

They walked up to the tunnel and jumped onto the path, which took them, a little more slowly this time, back to the road.

"Did you find the trip interesting?" Starmol asked the boys. "Have you any more questions?"

Archie and Findley looked at each other. Yes, there was one question burning in their

minds. "Where are the boys?"

Chapter Six

A Visit to the Dragon Stables

Starmol laughed. "The answer to that question is simple. There are none."

"What! No boys at all?" Findley worried.

"Why not?" demanded Archie.

"Ah well now, that question is much more difficult to answer. There are a variety of reasons, and they all involve more history."

Findley groaned.

"All right Findley. The answer will keep. You've had enough lessons for now. I'll take you to see some other parts of our Wheel."

Together, they mounted the auto stairs, which took them down to the tunnel leading to the moving road. Starmol turned to Archie.

"What would you like to see Archie?"

"Hyeke said those round buildings are Rearer's houses. What are Rearers? Can we see some?"

"Rearers are people like us, but also quite special. They are chosen."

"Chosen?" queried Archie.

"Naturally. It is a very important job they have to do, and they must be of the right temperament."

"What job?" Findley wanted to know.

"They look after and rear the children. Only the most suitable people are given a child. They are very carefully selected."

"What sort of people?" Archie wondered.

"Couples electing to stay with each other for life, who want to give twenty years to rearing a child. The gift can never be withdrawn, or ended, except by severe illness, of which we have very little now, or death."

"How do you know how to find the right people? Archie asked her.

"Our Controllers have been selecting people with the best characteristics for child rearing for a very long time now. They know what flaws to look out for, and have an instinct for choosing exactly the right people.

For example, they never choose couples who have been together for less than five years."

"Why is that? In our world, people often have children before they are married."

"That may be so, Archie. I think that is very sad. We believe parents must be fully adjusted to each other, before they take on such a huge responsibility, and if the couple have been together for more than five years, they are obviously well adjusted and capable of loving and caring for a child."

"Couples? Two women you mean?" giggled Findley.

"Well naturally, we are all females here."

"Why is that?" Archie demanded, "Why aren't there any men?"

"When our ancestors in the survival farms underground realised that the males were becoming infertile..."

"What!" Archie was startled. "How could that be?"

"You probably do not realise this Archie, but your ability to father a child is actually already twenty-five per cent less than your father's was at your age."

"How can that be?"

"We believe there are various reasons for the decline."

"Such as what?" Findley wanted to know as much as Archie did. This conversation was becoming just a bit worrying.

"A major cause, we believe, was the chemicals used in the production of plastic drink containers. Over time, it gradually leached into the water, and eventually into rivers and even into the seas and oceans. It was all part of the bigger picture of pollution and affected other species besides man.

Fishermen began to find sea creatures that had mutated, born without fins, some not capable of reproduction, turtles were choked by plastic bags which they mistook for their favourite food, jellyfish. Other fish consumed the particles of bio degraded plastic, which was then in the flesh of the food the people were eating.

Man made materials such as plastics, in particular were a huge problem and affected your dimension very seriously. A great part of the water stored underground in case of war, was in large plastic tanks, and that did nothing to help man's infertility either."

"So they really did use cheap plastic?" Archie said.

"In many cases, yes, I regret to say." Starmol answered him.

"How did everyone survive so long then?" Findley was sceptical, not quite believing what he was being told.

"By the time the problem was recognised, in many cases it was too late, and the underground farms died out. Fortunately, some of them had fresh water from deep rivers, like ours, and others had their water stored in glass containers, so it was perfectly safe to use and recycle. Technologists and scientists, working on the infertility problem were able to make babies in test tubes, and for some reason that we've been unable to discover, the female babies were the only successful ones."

"So that is why babies are so important?"

"Well of course, Findley, there would be no future for the human race without them, would there?" Starmol was surprised at his question.

"What happens if a Rearer dies?" asked Findley

"A Grandma Rearer is chosen from the most successful retired Rearers. When Hyeke returns, I will ask her to take you over to look around a Rearer's house. Now, what about seeing some drama, or going outside to see one of the farms, or perhaps you are more interested in sport?" she asked them.

"Sport!" they chorused.

"That's fine. Hop onto the road then. It is the next stop. I will take you to see Brentolly. She will show you round. I will ask her to show you the stadium, and perhaps the stables."

"Stables! Do you have horses here then?" asked Findley.

"No, but we have some animals that you might find interesting. We are quite proud of our dragons."

"Dragons!"

"Huh! There's no such thing!" Findley sneered, "They are just a legend. Isn't that right Arch?" he turned to his friend for confirmation.

"I don't think so actually Fin, Archie replied. "There were lots of fossils of dinosaurs with wings, pterodactyls, things like that. I suppose they could have evolved too?"

He looked at enquiringly at Starmol who had been following their conversation with quiet fascination.

"Yes Archie, they could have been some sort of mutation from the Komodo dragons."

"But they are really fierce and only eat meat." Findley argued.

"Well Findley," Starmol told him, "Like us they had to adapt to survive too. Anyway, you would not recognise them now. Do you want to see them?"

"Yes. Please." Archie agreed quickly before Findley could say no, his friend could be a bit of a wuss sometimes and he was not going to miss a chance like this.

"Is it safe outside then?" Findley asked, worried.

"We have been having a very calm period over the last few weeks, I am happy to say, so I do not think you have to worry." Starmol smiled at Findley.

"How did you find the dragons? Were they on the surface when your relatives came up for the first time?" asked Archie.

"No, we had been settled up here for some time before one of the farmers found a dragon when she was checking her fields. It was a female and she had been quite badly injured when she flew into our dimension accidentally through a time funnel. It had closed behind her and she couldn't get back to her time.

The farmer took her back to the farmhouse and cared for her. She named the dragon Princess Graylyn. Shortly after she had settled in, the little dragon produced a clutch of eight beautiful eggs. They were all different colours."

"What happened to them?" Findley asked, interested in spite of still feeling a bit scared at the thought that he was actually going to see some dragons.

Starmol answered the boy, "The farmer knew she had found something special, the little pink dragon was an important find, and she asked Marietta, who was Controller at the time, if she could keep her at her house until the eggs hatched.

Marietta agreed, but told her the dragon must always be free to fly whenever she needed to."

"What happened to the eggs?" Findley wanted to know.

"Princess Graylyn kept them warm until they were all hatched safely, but the strain proved too much for her. She never really recovered from her injuries, and the farmer believed she was pining for her mate, who had been left behind in her dimension. One day she came home and found that Princess Graylyn had died."

"Oh, how sad, those poor chicks!"

"Not chicks, Findley, Dragonets! That is what baby dragons are called." Starmol told him.

"Fortunately, they were all safely reared by the farmer and allowed to fly free as she had promised Princess Graylyn. In return, they are our friends. This was quite a long time ago, you understand, and we have had several generations of dragons since then. In fact our head stable keeper was telling me there is a new clutch hatching very soon. Come along. I'll take you to the stadium now."

"Stadium?" wondered Archie.

"That is where the stables are." she explained.

"What about Hyeke? When is she coming to take us back?" Findley asked anxiously as he stepped onto the Ring road with Archie.

"Don't worry so much, she will be back before too long. Oh look, here is Brentolly coming to meet you now."

The road was slowing down at a large platform. They stepped off the road and stared at the woman waiting for them.

"It is good to see you." The boys heard her deep voice in their heads in surprise. She looked like a Grecian goddess. All golden brown, with jet black hair, tall and well muscled, but her voice was husky and dark.

"Like a man." thought Findley.

Brentolly answered him, "I would not know. We have no men here."

Findley went hot with embarrassment.

Archie had overheard his thought too. "Steady on Findley! He admonished his friend, "You must be more careful."

Findley looked chastened. "Sorry, didn't think! I mean..."

"Forget it!" Archie sent the thought abruptly and promptly forgot all about him. He was studying Brentolly. He noticed her body seemed extremely fit, with strong arms and legs. She was dressed in some blue, tough looking shiny material, fashioned into a short tunic.

He looked at her trainers in disbelief. They were the same as his! No. They just looked the same, he realised. On closer examination he could see the shoes had the same type of protective cushions around the ankles as the shuttle seats had.

"Brilliant!" he thought, "I must have a pair of those."

He was careful not to let Brentolly see his longing for her cool trainers. He was for sure not going to dig himself into Findley's mess.

Brentolly's voice in his head stopped his musings. "We are going to the stadium first, it is just through here."

Archie could see a short tunnel, similar to the others that accessed the Rings. They arrived at a wide flight of steps, which moved upwards transporting them quickly to the top.

"I wish our stairs at home moved like this!" Findley thought.

Archie grinned at him. "It's a good thing they don't! You would only get fatter!"

The stairs stopped and they found themselves at the entrance of an enormous oval stadium.

The light up here was extremely bright and Brentolly told them to put on their eye protectors. They hastily donned the magic sun-glasses, and looked about.

They could see seats covered all sides down to a grassed area, which was marked out in different sections of yellow.

"It is canary yellow grass!" Archie noticed, astounded. "How cool is that?" he noticed a narrow, pink path, about a metre wide, running around the perimeter.

"There's nobody here, Archie." Findley whispered.

Archie nodded and noticed Brentolly looking a bit confused. "What is the matter?" he asked her, back in thought transference mode. Her face cleared and she answered him. "It's nothing. I just lost touch for a second or two."

Oh oh! Archie thought to himself, working it out rapidly. They can overhear us when we send thoughts to each other, but they can't read what we are thinking, and it looks as if whispering is something they cannot understand. That's interesting. I must tell Findley later.

"We thought there would be people here." Findley was disappointed. "Where is everybody?"

"They are at the far end of the stadium, over there." Brentolly pointed.

In the distance, the boys could just make out people and animals moving about.

"Are they horses?" Findley asked "They are too far away to see properly."

"No," Brentolly laughed, "I told you we do not have any horses here. Those are dragons. They are waiting for you to join them. Step onto the path and it will take you over there to where they are."

Archie and Findley needed no second bidding; they quickly jumped onto the pink rubbery path, and began to run. The path moved beneath them and slowly picked up speed. They were nearly out of breath when the path finally slowed as they reached the far end of the stadium.

Two girls waited, each holding the reins of a dragon.

"What beautiful animals," panted Archie, breathless from his exercise; he was stunned. "They look exactly like the dragons of myths and legends in our time. I never ever would have believed such wonderful creatures could actually exist. They are amazing!"

"Do they bite?" asked Findley fearfully.

They heard the girls' laughter in their heads, even the dragons looked amused. "No. Not ever. Would you like a ride?"

"Wow really? Cool." Archie stepped forward, eagerly, and looked at the girls. One of them, the smaller of the two, who seemed to be in charge of the biggest dragon, handed her reins to him.

"What is his name?" he asked her.

"His name is Pantol. He is their Crystal Leader. I am Bettina, his Carer." she answered.

"Crystal?"

"Yes, that is what we call a group of dragons, because of all their brilliant colourings, as you can see from Pantol's lovely coat."

The dragon heard his name and his head swung slowly round to face Archie. Archie stood still and gazed into Pantol's eyes. The huge brown eyes, with long, curling eyelashes stared back at Archie, and he suddenly felt an overwhelming warmth and empathy for the animal. Without stopping to think, he threw his arms around Pantol's neck and hugged him.

"I can see you have already bonded." Bettina smiled.

Pantol's head was just a little higher than Archie's, and his body, although low, was quite long. His strong back legs reminded Archie of a kangaroo's, but his tail was much longer, and he had a bony crest that started on his head between his ears and went three-quarters of the way down his back. Instead of front legs, the dragon had wings, which were folded close to his sides. His body was covered with an iridescent green layer of soft velvety feathers. His nose was blue and Archie stroked it carefully, surprised at how soft and smooth it was. His ears, again like those of a kangaroo, were large, rounded and soft, standing up on his head.

Archie couldn't take his eyes off him. A small saddle was strapped to his back, above his back legs, and behind his wings. The reins he was holding were made of soft green leather, plaited around Pantol's head.

Findley was feeling a little braver now that he had seen Archie come to no harm. His dragon was a blaze of dark orange; his carer stepped forward.

"Here you are." She handed him the reins. "This is Landon, and I am Maryetta, his Carer. If you stand still here, I'll help you to mount him."

Findley glanced quickly over at Archie, who was still lost with wonder, and shrugging helplessly, he nodded.

Landon moved round, so that Findley could reach the saddle and squatted to assist him to mount. As he settled in the saddle, arm cushions expanded round his waist and held him securely in place.

"Magic!" he breathed. "Look at me!" Findley exclaimed out loud in his excitement, beaming as he sat up in the saddle.

Archie couldn't stop grinning as he mounted Pantol. He sent his thanks and delight to Bettina, as his eyes sparkling, he sat back and allowed the cushions to mould to his waist.

Findley carefully pulled on the reins, and turned Landon to come alongside. "Aren't they wonderful? This is fantastic!"

"Absolute class!" agreed Archie enthusiastically.

Suddenly, they were surrounded by several more dragons and riders.

"Hey! What's happening?" asked Findley in a fright at all the commotion.

"It's okay, we are all going over to The Shivering Forest. Come on." A chorus of thoughts assailed the boys. Disjointed words and sentences buzzed in their heads from every direction. Archie thought he heard the word 'flying'.

It seemed Findley had heard it too. Completely forgetting to thought transfer in his panic, he shouted to Archie, "Flying? Can dragons fly, Arch?"

"They've got wings, haven't they? I've a feeling we shall find out, but I bet they can."

The carers stepped forward and murmured goodbye to the dragons. Findley leaned forward in his saddle, suddenly afraid.

"I can't ride," he thought desperately. "I can't even ride a horse."

"Do not be frightened," said Maryetta, "You are perfectly safe. You can't fall off, and the dragons know what to do. All you have to do is sit still and enjoy the ride. Goodbye for now. We will see you later when you bring the dragons back."

She and Bettina stepped back, and Pantol and Landon gathered themselves together and began to run on their strong legs, alongside the other dragons, whose riders had waited to watch the new recruits.

Archie and even Findley were so excited, absolutely thrilled to be trusted with these fabulous animals. They leaned forward, copying the others who were holding their reins wrapped around the crests on their dragons' backs.

"It feels a bit bumpy, like when I was on holiday in Egypt with Mum, and had a go on a camel." Findley thought.

Archie, who had never been on any animal in his life, thought his dragon was the coolest dragon on the planet, and for sure he was the most comfortable.

As he was thinking this, he felt a heavy warm glow go right through his body, and he realised with awe that Pantol knew just what he was thinking!

This is just the best day ever! thought Archie to himself in delight.

The dragons raced though the wide open gates of the stadium to the outside, and Archie could see they were running in a huge area of cultivated fields, criss-crossed by narrow paths of beaten earth. A bit like the farms at home, he thought, but smaller fields.

Far off to their left, outside the stadium Archie could see several huge glass domes, not high, but covering some metres; and he wondered what they were.

One of the riders dropped back to answer him. "Those are our schools," he told Archie, "There are three, Primary, Secondary and Tertiary. We are very proud of our schools. We have been lucky enough to produce some of the best at Wheel Trell, we have created scientists and technologists far more advanced than any of the other Wheels, and our graduates are in great demand by Clunn who have very few inhabitants, and who need all the help they can get."

"How do they teach the children here?" he asked "Do they have computers?"

"I believe they have something along those lines now, I am not sure, but each child is taught at her own pace, and they use a virtual system. They have regular discussions until they are twelve, about which area of Artrossian life, they want to enter. It could be anything from tending the farms, looking after the town 'Down', working in the hospitals, or maintenance. Whatever they want to do can usually be arranged, and from then on they are attached to their chosen area to learn more.

"Like apprentices." Archie thought. "Which is considered the best job, I wonder?"

"I think my job is the best, looking after the dragons, and riding out to make sure we are all safe. But everyone thinks they have the best job. That is the beauty of our training. It ensures that every-one is happy, no matter what they choose to do. We all have different strengths. My name is Lawrie, by the way, and this is Teddius." Her dragon was blue, and a little smaller than Pantol.

Archie looked down, the schools had been left far behind and they were approaching what appeared to be a huge hole in the ground. "What is that?" he asked her, pointing towards the ground. They were flying over a great white area, of what looked like stone or chalk. In the centre, Archie could see a large sparkling building; it seemed to have a many-faceted spire and although it was quite wide, it did not seem very high. In fact the top of the spire just reached the top of the quarry walls.

Lawrie looked where he was pointing and told him, "That is our new project. We are in the middle of building it. When it is finished, it will be a special place where anyone can go for a silent time."

"Silent time?" queried Archie.

"Yes. In our society it is considered quite rude to shut off thought transference, which means some people never get time for peaceful reflection. One of our Controllers had this idea, and we are looking forward to when the project is finished.

"I suppose it will be a bit like a cathedral." Archie thought. "What a good idea."

"Not a cathedral, no, nor a Mosque, or a Synagogue, I know they are places of worship in your Dimension, but this is not to be for that purpose. We all need a place of peace and serenity sometimes, and this is all the building will be used for.

When it is finished, there will be many individual rooms, and people will be able to stay for as long as they wish, a few minutes or several hours. It will be entirely their choice. All thought transference will be switched off. Anyone will be able to go there to restore their inner balance."

Gradually, they left the evidence of civilisation behind them and were soon out in the rough, uncultivated area of Wheel Trell.

Far into the distance, Archie could see a green haze on the horizon, and guessed that must be where they were headed.

The Shivering Forest! The name conjured up hints of mystery. He wondered what sort of animals lived there, and could scarcely contain his anticipation. He looked across at Findley, who seemed to have recovered from his earlier fears and was grinning all over his face.

Several thoughts reached him at once, taking him by surprise. "Swamp ahead!" came from the front riders. No sooner had Archie taken in and understood the meaning of the words, when as one, all the dragons unfurled their wings and jumped into the air, and he saw their wings were beautiful, made up of millions of tiny feathers, sparkling and gleaming in the bright sunlight.

Archie's heart was racing, the feeling of the warm scented air rushing past his face, made him feel more alive than he ever had before. He looked down at the ground rushing along beneath him and just knew that this was the best moment of his life. He wanted it to go on and on.

He looked over at Findley, flying alongside him, flung his arm into the air and yelled out loud with sheer exhilaration. "Yeeessss!"

"Wow! This is the best ride ever!" cried Findley "It's wild, man!" He excitedly returned Archie's salute. The other riders grinned at them and waved. Then:

"Hold on tight. It looks like rough weather is coming our way." A rider on Archie's left pointed over to the West. Archie looked across and could see a huge black cloud, hovering over the grass. It seemed to be advancing at an enormous speed, with lightning sparking from it in all directions.

The dragons slowed down as it approached. A rider dropped back and came alongside as the boys exchanged frightened looks.

"It will be all right, the storm is going so fast it will pass right in front of us."

Archie looked across at the girl and thought "I certainly hope so, it looks pretty evil to me."

"Yes, they can cause dreadful damage," the girl agreed, "but this is only a little one, and it will miss us, I promise you Archie. See how the dragons are all slowing down. They know it has to be allowed to pass in front."

Archie grinned at her "You know my name, but I do not know yours. Hardly seems fair. Does it?"

"My name is Jessacal, my friends call me Jessa. This is Elanora." She gestured proudly towards her dragon. "Isn't she lovely?"

Archie agreed with her that her pink, velvety skinned lady dragon was indeed lovely, but not, he thought to himself, a patch on his own steed. Once again he was rewarded with the warm heavy glow, and he squirmed in his seat in secret delight.

He wondered if all the riders had this sort of bond with their dragons, and a thought came into his head that was so startling, that if he had not been safety cushioned into his saddle, he might have fallen off.

"Did you speak to me?" in utmost amazement, he asked Pantol.

His dragon's head nodded, and in his head he heard;

"Super bonding is very rare. Do not worry your head about it, Archie, none of the others can hear us."

Archie was nearly beside himself with wonder. Findley's dragon drew alongside and the boys leaned towards each other and exchanged high fives. They could not believe they were actually flying!

The storm cloud was coming up to them faster now, and Findley kept glancing nervously over at it, afraid they were going to be hit. It certainly looked very close now.

"It is going to be okay." said Archie, "Don't worry, the storm is going to miss us."

"How do you know?" Findley asked. "What about the stadium?"

Jessa answered him. "Don't worry so, Findley. "If it goes towards the stadium, they'll put the Protectors over, no problem."

"Protectors?" Archie raised his eyebrows querying.

"They are shields that roll right across and cover the whole stadium. When the weather is bad or the sun is too bright, the Protector Canopies automatically cover the stadium, gardens and all the other small areas. Apart from the farms, but our cereals can withstand most of what the weather throws at us." Jessa explained.

"Cereals?" asked Archie, as they watched the ominous black cloud pass them by. The dragons flew in lazy circles, well out of reach of the storm, as their riders chatted nonchalantly among themselves, whilst waiting for it to go safely into the distance.

"I suppose everything you grow has been genetically engineered, like the grass outside your Wheel?" he asked.

"Yes, but it is quite safe. Our scientists have managed to keep all the flavour and nutrients of the plants, while breeding in strength to withstand the winds. Our corn stands just above the ground, very little stalk so it doesn't get flattened, and the ears are able to ripen more quickly.

Each stem has multiple ears too, so they would take up less space when grown underground."

"What about cattle, do you have cows?"

"No, but we do have sheep, and rabbits, for milk, meat and wool. We are really lucky, most of our problems have been solved for us. Well... she looked at Archie "All but the biggest problem, that is..."

Archie thought he knew what she was referring to, but decided not to take the bait. The storm had gone now, and the trees were in full view; and from this distance, they looked spectacular. They appeared to be shimmering in the sunshine.

"What beautiful trees." he asked "What makes them tremble like that?"

Jessa told him. "When you arrive and land, have a good look at the leaves. They are round and very light, with long stalks attaching them to the branches, so they move and twirl at the slightest breath of air. All of them moving together are a wonderful sight. That is why it's called the Shivering Forest. In the autumn they are all different colours; absolutely beautiful. But more importantly, they tell us when there is a disturbance in the ground, earth tremors, for example."

"Earthquakes?" Archie asked, surprised. "I thought the planet had stabilised itself."

"It almost has. The tremors are very few now, only one or two every year or so."

"One or two earthquakes a year!" Archie was shocked, "That is a huge number!"

"Oh no, it really is not," Jessa argued. "Only fifty or sixty years ago, they used to have two or three a month, and it made things very difficult for our people who worked outside, because the earthquakes are always accompanied by terrible storms. Things are a great deal better now that there are not so many, but that is why the Shivering Forest is so important to us."

"How can the trees help?" Findley had been listening, and was a little bit scared there might be an earthquake while they were outside.

"The quakes usually begin with very slight tremors that gradually build up over two or three days, as soon as this starts, the leaves tremble violently, making a sighing sound, which can be heard for several miles, giving us plenty of warning of an oncoming earthquake and storms.

That is why we regularly ride this way. Just to make sure all is well, as it is today."

"What about winter, when there are no leaves on the trees?" Findley wanted to know.

"There are always some leaves on the trees, they grow all the year round, except in really exceptional weather, and we've already gone 'Down' by then." Jessa assured him.

"We'll be landing soon."

Another rider dropped back to talk to the boys.

"Hi! My name is Brritt. The trees are normal today, so we are going to stop and have some food in a minute."

"What about that big black storm cloud we saw on the way here, just now?" asked Findley, still secretly worried.

"Oh, we have those all the time. They are nothing to worry about."

Findley was not so sure. If that storm cloud was nothing to worry about, he thought to himself, what were the storms they did worry about look like?"

Brritt had turned her attention to her dragon, which was slowly dropping down into a clearing in the trees.

Pantol and Landon followed, landing lightly on the ground and stopping at the edge of the wood.

"The saddle cushions released the boys and they dismounted, keeping a tight hold on the reins. Pantol told Archie the dragons were usually encouraged to walk freely through the Shivering Forest in search of their favourite titbit, lichen, or moss that lived on the trees, while the riders had their meal.

Sure enough the riders released their dragons, tying the reins safely to their crests, and sending them off into the trees for their treats.

Archie watched as the hampers were opened and identical boxes, each bearing a name, were handed out.

"Here you are Archie, and there is one for you too Findley." Jessa said, passing them their boxes. "The maitre'd sent these for you, based on what you looked at this morning. I hope they are okay."

"How did you know we would be coming with you?" Archie demanded.

The girls exchanged embarrassed glances, "Brentolly thought you might, so we packed some food for you just in case."

"I think she knew you would not be able to resist a ride on a dragon!" Brritt added.

Not really in a position to argue, the boys opened their boxes.

"Hey! Bramble pie!" shouted Findley, "My favourite! Oh sorry!" he sent the thought, "I keep forgetting!" The girls smiled at him forgivingly and understanding his excitement.

Archie smiled too, as long as Fin had food, he was happy. He looked in his own box and was not surprised to see some of his own favourites. He loved egg mayonnaise sandwiches. He started eating with approval.

Every-one was quiet as they ate steadily. Archie could hear Pantol murmuring his pleasure as he found a rare tasty titbit. He could not believe his luck that he could actually hear him.

Archie finished his food and leaned back against a tree. He felt quite tired, and he noticed one or two of the other riders were also settling down, when they had finished eating. He closed his eyes, ready to take a short nap to refresh himself.

It was then that he felt it. It was a terrible, cold, sick feeling of horrid dread; deep in the pit of his stomach. At first he thought he must have been poisoned, then he remembered the last time he had this feeling. He could only ever recall having it once in his life before.

He shivered, remembering. It was his twin sister Emmaline's and his eighth birthday. His mother had taken Emma to the swimming pool for her birthday treat, for some swimming lessons, and he'd gone to a football match with his father.

Archie knew immediately, as he had then, that something awful had happened to his sister. On the last occasion, she had been dragged unconscious from the pool, after a diver had landed on her. He had managed to persuade his father to leave the match, and go to the pool, where they had found a lifeguard giving Emmaline the kiss of life. As they approached he told Archie's parents, there was no hope, she had been in the water too long.

He sat, leaning against the tree, remembering how he had knelt down beside her, and held her in his arms and whispered into her ear, using their own special language, talking, and cajoling for what seemed hours, until she knew he was there and had opened her eyes, and made a complete recovery.

Archie felt sick. What on earth could she be doing here? He decided Murray must have brought her with him. They must have found the funnel in the cottage. Honestly! Sometimes he thought his stepbrother had no sense at all. This time he had really done it.

He must have seen us step onto that carpet, he thought, and followed them to Artross.

But what could be wrong? Everybody had been so good to Findley and himself.

Was that why Hyeke had gone off and left them so suddenly? Had they been packed off here to be out of the way, while they decided what to do with Emmaline? Because it was for sure she would not be welcome, they already had a surfeit of girls!

Archie felt ill, how could he help her, stuck as he was, away out here? He could tell she was under some form of restraint. He wondered if she could receive thought messages, and was about to try to send her one, when he realised no-one had told him she was here.

Any attempt by him to send any thoughts would be picked up by one or maybe all the girls he was sitting with, and they would then be alerted to the fact that he knew his sister was here, and keep a watch on him.

What on earth was he to do? What could he do?

In a flash, the answer came to him. Pantol would help, yes, he was sure of it. He leaned forward and gently touched Findley's arm.

Findley looked over and thought "The food is fantastic, isn't it Arch?"

Archie nodded, and whispered softly to him. "Don't talk. Don't think. Especially don't think. They can understand us when we talk in telepathy, even just to each other. They can also hear us when we talk out loud, but whispering confuses them. Remember Brentolly?"

Findley nodded, carefully chewing his apple.

"Emmaline is here somewhere, and I think Murray is too. That must have been the 'little matter' Hyeke had to attend to. I think Emma is in trouble and I have to try and help her.

I'm going for a ride on Pantol, okay. Not a word to them." Archie looked up. His whispers had caught their attention. Several riders were watching him, looking puzzled.

He flashed them a smile, and sent them by telepathy, "Sorry. I forgot, I was just telling Findley about the nice things in my food box."

They relaxed and continued eating and dozing.

Chapter Seven

Emmaline is in Trouble

Archie stood up. "Is it okay if I take my dragon for a ride? I'd like to see more of your beautiful countryside, and perhaps take a look at some of the farms."

Jessa scrambled to her feet, and took his arm. "I will take you."

Gently, Archie lifted her hand away. "Not just now, thanks Jessa, I'll find my own way. Solitude is a boy thing, you understand?"

Jessa blushed but sat down quickly, saying, "Okay we'll be here for a couple of hours yet."

"Good." Archie sighed with relief. He winked at Findley and sending the thought that he would see them all later, he walked confidently away into the trees.

Pantol was waiting just out of sight of the others. Quickly Archie explained to the dragon. "We need to find my sister. I know she's in trouble somewhere nearby. Have you any idea where she could be?"

"Regretfully not." Pantol shook his head sadly. *"Archie are you sure she is here? How do you know this?"*

Archie explained to the dragon as they walked back out of the wood. He told him about the horrid feeling in his stomach, and that the only time he had ever felt that way before was when Emmaline was nearly drowned.

Pantol agreed with Archie that it did seem very bad, and he would help him if he could.

When they arrived at a grassy patch outside the wood; well away from the others, Pantol squatted down to assist the boy to mount. As he settled back in the saddle, Archie asked him to fly over to the Rearer's houses, but to keep out of sight when they got there.

"Why do you think she may be located there?" Pantol asked him.

"It's only a guess, but the Rearer's homes are near the entrance to the time funnel from my place. I know she would not be welcome here, because she is a girl, and that means they probably will not have bothered to take her very far. That is what I'm hoping, anyway.

I am fairly sure she will be somewhere in that area. When we get nearer I shall try and contact her with telepathy. It is possible Hyeke would have unlocked that part of her brain at the same time she unlocked Murray's."

Pantol was worried. *"That makes a great deal of sense, Archie, but you do realise if you attempt to contact her, your thoughts can be picked up by the Artrossians?"*

"Yes, I do know that, Pantol." Archie tried to soothe the dragon's fears. "I found that out by accident. It cannot be helped though, I must make contact, or we will never find her. You know, although the Artrossians have been very good to us, I can't help feeling that they seem to have imprisoned my sister. I shall use our baby language, which hopefully they will not understand."

"But they will know you are communicating." The kindly dragon was not convinced.

Archie sighed. "I know Pantol. I'll just have to hope that we can escape before they catch us. Is it much further?"

They had been flying now for about half an hour, and the horrid feeling that had alerted Archie to Emmaline's predicament was not abating and he was very worried.

"About twenty more minutes before we can see the homes. Try and relax, Archie and enjoy your ride." Pantol advised him.

"What is your history, Pantol? Starmol told us about Princess Graylyn, and the first clutch of eggs in Wheel Trell. You must be descended from her. Were you bred for riding by the females?" Archie asked him.

"No, no. We are not bred by them at all. We are entirely independent, although some of us live in the stadium at egg-laying time. It is much more secure for the hatchlings' safety.

Our being on Wheel Trell is relatively recent. We evolved outside in another dimension, while the females here were still living Down.

We believe Princess Grayling died because she was outside her own time for too long, but her eggs hatched in this dimension, so they were able to thrive, and breed here.

There are actually many smaller animals on the surface here now, but we are the largest."

"When I was in the bubble with Findley, we saw an enormous creature that Hyeke said must be a raptorvor. Are there many of those around here? The one we saw was huge!" Archie said.

"I know which animal you mean." Pantol sneezed loudly. *"Sorry. A reaction to the pollen from that field, I believe the farmer down there is trying a new plant this season.*

Where was I? Oh yes, the raptorvor is harmless, he only eats vegetation, although like us he was probably a meat eater in the past, or rather his ancestors were. He was probably attracted by the bubble. They usually only come out at night, and are quite timid."

"What do you eat?" Archie asked, "Besides moss, I mean." Pantol snorted, and Archie understood that the dragon was amused.

"Anything at all edible usually. Mostly grass and leaves, but any vegetables are welcome. I'm afraid we ate a good bit of the Artrossian's harvests, before we came to a mutual understanding."

"Oh?" Archie nodded, "How did that work?"

"With bartering, a fair exchange. We help them with the heavy work and they give us extra food. But they understand that we are not their servants, any more than they are ours."

"So you live comfortably together?" Archie thought. "That is so sensible. Do you know how many dragons there are on Artross, now Pantol? Have many super-bonded, like us?"

"There is a small Crystal of dragons living far away in the mountains, North of Wheel Trell, but they rarely venture this far." The dragon told him.

"They have little contact with us, so I cannot speak for them, but to answer your question about super-bonding, I know of only six in all. In fact not for many, many years has it happened, until you and me today."

"Why do you think that is?" Archie queried.

"In recent years there has been an undercurrent of feeling. Unfortunately not all of the Artrossians agree on a certain course of action they are planning. About half are actively seeking ways to introduce males into their lives again.

All of my family have taken the decision not to become involved if they begin to fight, so we will not bond with any of them until the issue is safely resolved, one way or another."

"I see." said Archie, he had a bad feeling about all this; a quiet dread crept over him, as he began to understand.

"Is that why we are being treated so well? They want us to stay?"

"I can tell you this Archie. When you arrived, the whole wheel knew you were boys within seconds. Some of the Artrossians want to keep you here by force, if necessary; and the others are against keeping you if you don't want to stay. Try not to worry about it now," the dragon told him quietly.

"Elanora has just told me your group of riders have been looking for us, and have decided to fly back to the stadium to report on your disappearance."

"Oh no," moaned Archie, "I thought we would have some more time."

"They are worried about us, and are thinking of sending out a search party, hopefully they will not think of this direction just yet, as it is quite some way from the farms you told them you wanted to visit. Now Archie, see in front down to the left?"

Archie looked down and could see tiny round white balls nestled into the grass. From where he sat, they looked like his uncle's golf balls.

"Those are the outer Rearer's homes, where the older children are. I shall go higher now, and skirt round to the other side where the steps are." Pantol's wings beat fiercely taking them soaring up into the sky.

Archie could feel the scorching heat of the sun, and was glad of the protector band he still wore over his eyes.

Looking down, he could just make out the amphitheatre where (was it only this morning?) Hyeke had taken him and Findley down to the Ring road. He knew with absolute certainty that his twin Emmaline was down there somewhere, he could feel her presence. He told Pantol, who agreed.

"I am going to fly in a spiral down from right above the steps, so hopefully we will not be seen."

Archie held tightly onto the dragon's bumpy crest before him, the reins wrapped securely around his hands, as Pantol flew in tight ever decreasing circles. "Emmaline!" Archie called out to her with his thoughts concentrated on her, desperately hoping she would hear him.

"Archie! Help me, help me, they have locked me in a cage. I can't get out." Her frightened voice nearly lifted Archie's head off, and Pantol heard it too.

"Ask her where she is." he directed Archie. They heard her immediate response to his question, and Archie guessed she could hear Pantol as well as he could.

"The cage is standing on some steps. Please hurry, Archie, it's so hot."

The dragon quickly changed direction and veered off, diving down to the side steps, softly alighting near a large metal cage.

"Archie!" Emmaline shrieked with relief when she saw her brother.

Archie lifted his finger to his lips, and whispered. "Hush Emma, do not speak, or even think; we haven't much time. I'm afraid they will find us before very long. Now, how can we get you out?"

He slid off Pantol's back, and walked around the cage, looking for a door. "I can't find a way in. Where is the door? How did you get in there?" he whispered anxiously. He felt a nudge in his back, and turned round.

Pantol told him, *"Tell your sister to stand away from the sides."*

Emmaline understood the dragon and was scared, but moved quickly towards the back.

"What are you going to do?" she whispered.

Pantol answered her by slowly drawing in a long, deep breath. He held it for a few seconds, and Archie was alarmed to see Pantol's cheeks puff up and begin to glow a bright fiery red. Smoke began to pour from the dragon's nostrils. All at once, he directed his head at the metal cage, well away from Emmaline, and opened his mouth with a fearsome roar. Hot flames spouted from Pantol's mouth, directly over the cage; gradually, the metal melted, and soon, a large hole appeared. Pantol stopped breathing fire and stood aside, so that Emma could get out.

"Careful, the bars are still hot," Archie said, as he helped his sister. When she was safely out, he gave her a hug. She was looking at the dragon with big scared eyes.

"It's okay Emmaline," whispered Archie, "This is Pantol and he's a friend, he has helped me to find you, and he's taking us back the way you came in."

"Archie, why are you whispering? There is nobody here; they said no-one wanted me." Emmaline started to cry.

"Hush now, I have to whisper because if we talk or send thoughts to one another, we can be overheard, I have discovered that they cannot understand us when we whisper. Now we have to get you back."

"Oh Archie, Emmaline whispered, holding tightly on to her brother's hand, "I'm so glad you're here. What is this place? Who are those women who put me in that cage? Why did they do it?"

"I don't know yet Emmaline, but I mean to find out."

"Murray was with me and they took him away. Do you know where he is? I'm so frightened Archie."

"It's all right. Come on now, Murray will be okay, stop crying, I'll explain everything later but we mustn't waste time. We could be discovered at any moment. Be quick now, Emmaline. Here is your chance to have a wonderful ride on this beautiful dragon."

Archie was rewarded by a tremulous smile from his sister, as he helped her get on Pantol's back, before climbing up himself and settling unto the large saddle behind her. The cushions reached round and held them safely together.

"Go Pantol!" Archie breathed. The dragon needed no urging. Gathering himself, he launched his body high up into the air, way above the Rearer's homes.

"Where is the canopy?" worried Archie, looking down for the telltale bubble that was their way home. Pantol flew back and forth, searching.

"I know it has to be here somewhere," Archie said, frantically looking all around the fields. I know it has to be somewhere near here." he said to Emmaline. He thought for a moment.

"Pantol," he addressed the dragon. "It was next to the Rearer's home that is nearest to the amphitheatre. I remember; we walked past it this morning. Got it!" he said quickly "Hyeke said that bubble stuff goes down into the funnel to keep it open, so the canopy will no longer be there. Keep your eyes peeled, for a small hole in the ground, Emmaline. We are just about over it now.

As he spoke, Pantol veered down sharply to the right.

"There it is!" Emmaline pointed.

Suddenly Archie heard a cacophony of sound in his head, and looking behind, he saw to his horror, a whole group of women riding on dragons, almost upon them.

"There is no time for us to land and dismount, Pantol; we will all have to go down the funnel together."

Pantol bravely dove for the entrance, ignoring the leader of the pack of females behind him as she ordered him to stop.

They landed in an untidy heap on the carpet in the cottage.

Archie and Emmaline slowly picked themselves up from the floor and looked at each other.

Pantol was asleep nearby, his huge bulk blocking the close door.

Archie grabbed his sister's arm, and gave her a long, heartfelt hug. "Thank goodness we managed to find you, and get you back. You must get out now, Emmaline, where you'll be safe, okay? Go to Mum's and I'll see you there later, okay?" he smiled, "We've heaps to catch up on and talk about."

As Emmaline hesitated, he said urgently, "Hurry, Emmaline they'll follow us down here to get Pantol back. You must not be here then."

Emmaline looked around frantically, "Where can I hide? I can't get out!"

"Here let's see if the window will open this time." Archie went over to the window and struggled for a minute, before with an alarming creak, the window swung wide open. He pushed away the ivy clinging to the outside frames and said

"Come on, hurry up Emma, you must get out." He bumped her up to the low windowsill. She turned, looking back at him, as she crouched on the sill.

"Aren't you coming, Archie?"

"I can't, not yet." he argued.

"You must. It's dangerous up there!" she urged her brother, desperate for him not to go back into the funnel.

"I have to go back, Emma, I have to find Murray and Findley and help them to get back here safely, and Pantol must get back to his home too. Hurry *up!* Jump down, wait! Tell Findley's Mum he's staying with me tonight, and tell Mum I'm staying at Findley's house."

"Why?" she demanded.

"Listen, if you tell them the truth, they'll never believe you. Now, it may take a bit of time, to find every-one, and if we are late back, this way, no-one will worry. Understand?"

Emmaline smiled uncertainly.

"If I don't get back tonight, just go back to Dad's and I'll see you tomorrow, okay?"

Archie leaned forward and kissed her, giving her a gentle push. She turned and threw her arms around his neck, then kissed him back and let go, ready to jump from the sill and into the garden. "I am so sorry about... you know," she whispered, "We are all right again now aren't we?"

"Of course we are, go along now."

Archie watched her run down the path, happy that they were friends again. He had really missed having his sister in his life.

A noise behind him, made him turn back into the room. He was shocked to see Hyeke and Bettina, Pantol's carer, appear out of thin air in front of him.

"Bettina, Hyeke, what on earth are you doing here?" demanded Archie.

"We have come to apologise, Archie, we did not know she was your sister!" Hyeke put her arms out to Archie, appealing for forgiveness.

"It does not matter who she was. It was a disgraceful thing to do. I had begun to believe you were all so much more civilised than us, but it is all just for show, isn't it?" Archie was disgusted with her.

"No, no you must believe me..." Hyeke was scared. She had to make Archie return with her.

Bettina interrupted sharply "Please stop bickering, you two. I cannot wake Pantol. His colour is fading and he looks dreadful. We must get him back without any more delay. Where is the entrance?"

Archie ran over to his friend. He was very concerned for Pantol, and switched over to thought transference.

"Let me help. It is that bright piece of carpet over there." he pointed over to it, and the girls hurried to help him roll the dragon over onto the patch. Quite suddenly Pantol disappeared, and quick as a flash, Archie stepped onto the carpet and followed him with Bettina close behind and Hyeke following them.

The canopy was crowded with people. Archie looked round for Findley but he couldn't see him. "Where is Findley?" he asked, but nobody was interested, they were all looking with horror at Pantol, who lay unconscious on the grass.

Archie watched anxiously as a group of riders gently unbuckled the saddle, taking it carefully off his back, while Bettina carefully unwound the bridle and reins from his head. Then they slowly eased Pantol onto a large canvas like sheet, securing him to it with soft restraining straps. The riders then attached strong, wide straps to the sides and corners of the sheet, and looped the other ends, one to each of the dragons, around the bony crests on the backs of their necks.

Archie noticed Jessa was one of the riders, and her dragon Elanora, was weeping silent tears.

"Jessa." he pleaded, "Can I ride with you? Pantol is my friend and I must go with him."

Jessa looked at him listlessly. "If you feel you must, you are welcome to ride with me, but I fear it is far too late."

She mounted Elanora and indicated that he could sit behind her saddle. Archie climbed up, and the dragons set off, carefully keeping in step, so as not to jolt poor Pantol too much.

"Jessa, please tell me. What is wrong with him?" asked Archie, devastated that his friend was so ill.

"There were no dragons in your time, he could not live there." she shrugged her shoulders, crossly.

Archie was shattered, "Did he know that when he took us into the funnel?"

"Yes." she said sadly.

The boy was silent. He grieved for his brave friend, without whom, he knew, he would never have been able to rescue his sister. He looked across at Pantol lying on the sheet between the dragons, *"Hold on my friend,"* he thought, *"hold on."*

The dragons had slowed their pace. Archie could see they were arriving at a huge, wedge shaped building. It seemed to be rising up, out of the ground. The dragons stopped, and the large doors in the upright part of the building opened out wide.

The dragons walked slowly inside with their heavy load. The other riders and their dragons stayed outside the doors, watching in complete silence.

Archie slipped down from Elanora's back, and followed the dragon bearers into the building. He walked over to Pantol, and waited while the straps were removed, and Pantol was resting on a large soft mat on the floor.

Jessa walked over to where Archie stood waiting, trying to see if his friend was still breathing.

"What do we do now?" Archie asked her.

"There is nothing more we can do. We will leave him here tonight. You can come and see him in the morning, if he has recovered." she said to him, softly.

"No! There must be something we can do. You can't just leave him. Archie argued, urgently.

"It is the way things are. Now come. I will take you for something to eat." Jessa said, taking his arm.

"Take me for something to eat? Are you mad? How can you even think I would leave him for food? I couldn't eat a thing anyway, knowing he was lying here all alone. I shall stay with him tonight." Archie was getting angry.

"Stay with Pantol? Oh no, Archie, you cannot do that."

"And just why not?" Archie demanded aggressively.

"It, it is not usual." she said, looking at the others standing at the door, watching and waiting silently.

"That may be so, but where I come from, we do not desert our friends when they need us most. I am not moving from here. Okay? I am staying here with Pantol whether you and your people like it or not. That is my final word on the matter."

Faced with this ultimatum, Jessa knew when she was beaten. "Very well," she agreed, eventually, "But there is no light here."

Archie watched her walk to the door, where she turned and looked at him,

"You are sure?" she asked.

"I have never been so sure of anything in my life." Archie replied. She smiled at him, "You are very brave." she said as she went through the huge doors, and the riders pushed them closed, behind her.

"*Not brave at all*" he thought. He felt very alone in the dark. It was not just dark, he thought to himself fearfully, but absolutely pitch black. The blackness felt thick, as if it was choking him. He wondered what on earth this place was.

It certainly was not very comfortable. It was like a huge barn. He had noticed, before Jessa left that there were no windows, or any other openings, apart from the now firmly closed doors. The building had a cold empty feeling to it and he couldn't imagine what the Artrossians used it for.

He felt around on the floor, trying to make contact with the dragon. The riders had gently rolled Pantol off the canvas, and onto a soft looking rug, he remembered. He crept forward a little and bumped into Pantol's tail. He felt his way along the dragon's back until he could feel the bony crests, then he shuffled along on his knees until he arrived at the dragon's head.

Very slowly and carefully, so as not to disturb the dragon too much, he manoeuvred himself so he was sitting on the rug, with his legs stretched out, and Pantol's head was resting in his lap.

"Oh Pantol," he sighed. "I am so sorry, my dear friend." Archie stroked his hand across the dragon's nose and soft ears.

He was disturbed at how cold the animal's nose and ears were. He remembered how warm his ears had been before this dreadful thing happened. He stroked the nose and lovely soft ears, over and over again. "Please don't die, Pantol. I want to thank you for saving my sister Emmaline. She is very dear to me and we are friends again now. It is all due to you, I could never have saved her without you." he whispered. The dragon did not stir.

Archie ran his hands around the dragon's neck, rubbed vigorously over the bony crests. He stood up and, in the pitch black darkness, he massaged every inch of Pantol's body, over and over again, whispering to him how much he loved him, and he must not die, because he needed him too much.

Knowing Pantol was near death, and it was all his fault; exhausted with the adventures of the day and the over powering emotions he was discovering inside himself, Archie finally fell into a deep sleep, with the dragon's head in his lap, and his arms wrapped around his neck.

Archie awoke very early.

At first he could not think why he was sitting on a cold floor, and he thought he must have somehow fallen out of bed. Then he remembered.

It all came flooding back in a rush. He was with Pantol in some pitch black horrid barn of a place. He felt most indignant when he remembered that at first they had said he couldn't stay with his friend. It was still very dark, and he knew something had woken him.

He was startled to realise he was still holding Pantol's head in his lap; he felt the warmth of his breath on his knees. His legs had gone to sleep, from the weight of the dragon's head, and he tried gently to move them without disturbing him. Pins and needles prickled his legs and he stretched slowly. Pantol twitched in his sleep.

"I am so sorry, my friend for putting you into such terrible danger. Please forgive me, Pantol." Archie whispered.

As he felt the familiar golden warmth flood through his body, and realised Pantol was recovering, Archie felt the tears of thankfulness and joy run down his face. He was too slow to prevent them from splashing onto Pantol's nose.

"*Hey!*" he heard the faintest sound in his head. "*That's wet!*"

Laughing and crying at the same time, Archie pulled his legs free and scrambled around to hug the dragon. "You gave me such a fright!" he laughed, delighted.

"Would you like something to eat, or drink?" he added.

"*I am afraid you will not find any food or drinks in here, Archie.*" The dragon told him.

"Do you know where we are then?" Archie asked him.

"*I think we are in the Dying Chamber.*"

"What!" shouted Archie, shocked rigid. "You mean they just left us here because they thought you were dying? That's monstrous! That's ...that's just inhuman! Well, we had better jolly well let ourselves out of here, and the sooner the better, because we are definitely in the wrong place!" he stopped,

"Pantol, are you all right?" he asked anxiously. "I wish there was a light in this place. I wish I could see you. I can't believe they put dragons in here to die. It is horrific." Archie breathed a sigh of relief as Pantol's claws could be heard clattering on the hard floor.

"Where are you?" he put his hand out, and felt around in the dark, he could hear a rustling, and then the welcome sound of the doors opening automatically as Pantol leaned his weight against them hard. He walked quickly over to the exit, and dragon and boy stepped outside.

Dawn was just breaking, and the sky was filled with pink, creamy clouds. The sun was beginning to peep through on the horizon.

"How lovely it is at this time of day!" laughed Archie. "Hah! Listen to me! I'm usually asleep at this time of day."

"*We should go back to the stadium,*" Pantol suggested. "*They have taken my saddle and reins. Do you think you could manage to ride me bare-back?*"

"Are you strong enough to carry my weight yet? Archie asked him.

"*I am fine now, I have had a good sleep.*" he answered.

"Let's go then." Archie stepped up onto Pantol's knee as the dragon squatted to help him climb up. Archie swung his leg over the animal's back, and settled comfortably between two of the bony crests behind his wings, Pantol took a few steps, then, warning the boy to hold on tight, he launched himself up into the air.

As Pantol flew along steadily, to help the boy keep his balance, Archie heard the dragon sigh.

"What is wrong, Pantol?" he asked, concerned that his friend was still too weak for flying.

"Nothing is wrong, I am fine." Pantol told him. *"I was just thinking how good it will be to see my dragonets."*

"Dragonets?"

"Yes, my baby dragons, I should be with them, they will be missing me, but I am sure Jessa will be helping Elanora to care for them in my absence."

"Baby dragons? Oh Pantol, how lovely. How many do you have?"

"We have clutch of eight, this time. Elanora had just finished watching over the hatching before we went to the Shivering Forest yesterday.

It was her first ride for several weeks. I haven't seen them properly yet. Their feathers will be dry now, and we should be able to tell what colours they are."

"So you and Elanora are mates. I should have known." Archie said, remembering the lady dragon's tears when they had brought Pantol back from the tunnel.

A short time later, the two friends circled the stadium before Pantol lazily spiralled down to the end where Bettina was watching the other Carers attending to the needs of their charges.

Pantol hovered above her, and gently snorted.

Bettina swung round, startled, and her mouth fell open in wonder as she saw the dragon she was sure was dead, alight gently in front of her.

"Pantol! You're alive! How in the world..." she hurried over and stroked his nose lovingly.

"Archie! Are you all right? We were sure you'd...." her voice tailed away in his head as she watched Archie dismount.

"You were all sure what?" asked Archie.

"Oh, it's nothing Archie." Bettina said hurriedly and busied herself with a box of hay.

"They thought we would both be dead this morning," Pantol told him with amusement. *"Nobody ever volunteers to stay overnight in The Dying Chamber unless they are dying; so they were convinced you must be about to die too.*

You really shocked them Archie, staying there with me last night."

Archie patted the dragon's neck. "I am very glad I did stay with you." he turned to Bettina, "It is good to be back, Bettina, now how about some tasty vegetables for my friend? He must be starving, and thirsty." he added.

He watched while Bettina hurried to get a basket of titbits for Pantol, who had now completely recovered, and was drinking from a water bowl at the side of the wall.

The dragon raised his head, water streaming from his mouth, and turned to Archie. "Would you like to see the dragonets? He asked him "They are in the stable at the end. Just walk along and peep over the door."

Archie casually strolled too the end, and just as he came up t the door, Elanora put her head out over it. "She knows Pantol is all right." he thought, as he gently patted her nose. "Would you mind if I looked at your babies, please, Elanora? Pantol told me you have eight this time."

Elanora looked along the row of doors to her mate, who was watching Archie while tucking into some tasty nibbles. He nodded to her, and she withdrew her head and stood back. Archie leaned over the stable door. He could see a heap of fluffy, differently coloured tiny dragons, squirming about on a nest of soft feathers. One of them, bright pink, like her mother, struggled to stand up, and sneezed suddenly. She looked so surprised, Archie laughed.

"Oh, they're just beautiful Elanora."

Elanora huffed softly, as Pantol came up behind Archie. *"They'll be flying in a couple of weeks!"* he said proudly. *"We have been exceptionally lucky this time, Archie, we have royalty in this clutch! Two of the babies have hatched with the royal colours."*

"Royalty? What do you mean?" Archie looked at the dragonets "How do you know?"

Pantol said." *You see that one with the pinky-blue, lilac, lavender and cream coloured feathers?"* Archie nodded, fascinated with the lively bundle. *"She is a princess. All dragonets with those colours are princesses. There have only ever been three of these to my knowledge."*

"Wow! What will you call her?"

"Elanora and I have decided, when she is old enough, we will take her to see a very rare flower, which has the same colours as she does. It is the Hetharooth flower, and our daughter will be named after the flower, Princess Hetharooth."

Pantol beamed proudly, *"What do you think?"*

Archie said "I think it is a lovely name. Very regal." he leaned further over the door, "Which is the other one, Pantol? Oh, it must be the gold one. Am I right?" he turned his head and saw Pantol nodding.

"Yes, Archie, The golden one is a prince. He is the second one to be born in this dimension. He is to be named after Elanora's grandfather, Prince Krystoffer."

"I wish I could see them flying, Archie said, wistfully. "They are such lovely colours Pantol."

Pantol said to Archie. *"Perhaps you will. Who knows? However, in the meantime, you have other more pressing things to sort out now, and you should eat something, too."*

"Yes, I hope I will see you later, Elanora. Thank you for letting me see your babies, they are all beautiful." Elanora huffed softly as Archie gave Pantol a farewell hug.

"I will see you, too later, my friend."

"Why, where are you going?" asked Brentolly anxiously. Being the stadium manager, she had been alerted to unexpected arrival of Pantol and Archie, and had hurried over to see them.

"Hello, Brentolly." Archie said. "I have something I must do." he said airily.

"No, wait! I will come with you." Brentolly said desperately.

"What's the matter Brentolly?" Archie was scathing, "I won't get lost!"

He had not forgiven the females for leaving Pantol in the Dying Chamber.

Archie stepped quickly on to the pink perimeter path, and began running back to the tunnel where Brentolly had left he and Findley yesterday. He was not surprised to find Brentolly right behind him, when he arrived back at the tunnel entrance.

"Hi! Brentolly, there was really no need for you to follow me, you know, I will be fine on my own."

Brentolly smiled, "I'm quite sure you would be, Archie, but we cannot allow you to wander about our Wheel without some company. It would be most impolite. I was just about to get some breakfast. Would you like some?"

Archie was actually feeling ravenous, he had eaten nothing since the picnic in the Shivering Forest, and that was nearly a whole day ago! He smiled at Brentolly.

"Breakfast sounds good to me!"

Archie knew Brentolly must know of the events of the previous day, but she seemed oblivious, or perhaps she was just determined to pretend ignorance. Archie noticed she did not even enquire after Pantol's health.

"Pantol is fully recovered, by the way. I thought you would just like to know." he said. Brentolly did not answer him, and Archie wondered if these Artrossians had no feelings of empathy for the dragons at all.

He let Brentolly know what he was thinking, and she was stung into a reply.

"Of course we care for the dragons! How could you think we do not?" she stopped walking and faced him.

"Well! I really am glad to hear that." Archie said, "Your extraordinary custom of putting ill animals in the dying chamber all by themselves made me think otherwise. An easy enough mistake on my part, wouldn't you agree?"

"You do not understand our ways." Brentolly argued.

"Quite right Brentolly, I do not, nor would any right thinking human being!" Archie retorted angrily.

"You should speak to Starmol if you feel so strongly about it." said Brentolly, she was upset, "She can explain things."

"I do not need her to explain, I can think for myself. What can Starmol tell me anyway?" he demanded.

Poor Brentolly said desperately. "Listen, you know she is our Controller this week, if you talk to her, tell her how you feel; she may decide to change the laws about how we use the Dying Chamber."

"Could she do that?" Archie was interested, "Thanks Brentolly, I might just do what you suggest."

Friends again, they went off together to have some breakfast.

Chapter Eight

Archie Visits Hospital

Meals were being served to several families, as Archie and Brentolly entered with their discs after selecting from the menu.

As he sat at the table, eating as fast as he could, Archie thought about how he was going to find Findley and Murray. He really had no idea where they would be, and knew he would have to trust Brentolly, as she had obviously been directed to watch him.

"Don't eat so fast, Archie." Brentolly was looking at him anxiously, "You'll make yourself sick."

"I'm in a hurry." Archie snapped at her. "I have to find where your lot have stashed my friends and get us back to our own time, before the time funnel closes."

Brentolly sighed as she put her cutlery down.

"I do understand, Archie and don't think I don't sympathise with you, but I can certainly put your mind at rest about the time funnel. It has been temporarily reinforced, so you should not get trapped here."

"Well, that's one blessing, I suppose," grumbled Archie, as he watched the steam wand remove the evidence of his hasty meal.

He went to the restroom, and as instructed by Brentolly, pushed all his clothes into the hole in the wall, before stepping into the most luxurious shower he had ever been in. The warm soapy water vigorously massaged him, and then rinsed him in clear water. As he stood there, warm air caressed his skin, drying him thoroughly. Feeling refreshed and in a much better mood, he retrieved his clothes, clean, pressed and still slightly warm, and rapidly dressed, marvelling at the swift laundry service and wishing his mother could have a system like this. She always seemed to be ironing these days, he reflected, as he left the restroom and met up with Brentolly, who was patiently waiting for him.

"Where are we going?" Archie asked as they stepped onto the rolling Ring road.

"You want to find your friends, don't you Archie?"

"What have you done with them? Where are they?" he demanded, "Have you got them locked up somewhere? In a cage perhaps, like my sister?"

"That was most unfortunate..." Brentolly began.

"You're telling me! She might have died out there in that cage. Perhaps that was the idea? And all that trouble just because she is a girl!" Archie was scathing in his disgust of the treatment meted out to his sister.

"Please, Archie. We are not as bad as you seem to think. You must remember, we have not had to deal with this kind of thing before."

"Oh save it!" Archie scoffed. "A harmless girl? Really! My heart bleeds!"

"I am sorry your sister was frightened. She was only to be there a short time while we consulted with Starmol and she decided what to do with her." Brentolly's voice was hesitant in Archie's head.

"Why wasn't she treated the same way as Findley and me then?" demanded Archie.

"I cannot tell you. Starmol is Controller this week."

"Take me to her. Now!" demanded Archie.

"Very well. She can explain." Brentolly sounded relieved.

"Good! I should hope so too." Archie sounded brave, but in fact he was beginning to feel little niggle of worry.

He hadn't forgotten what Pantol told him yesterday. He wondered which side Starmol was on. Did she want to keep them there? Or were they to be allowed to return home?

In no time at all they had arrived at the Control Centre. As Archie stepped out of the shuttle, Starmol appeared on the platform.

"Good morning Archie, I trust you have recovered from your night in the Dying Chamber?" she nodded to Brentolly, and the girl quickly made her escape with relief. She liked Archie, but if truth were known, she was also a little afraid of him. Starmol took his arm and took Archie along to a small office at the side of the platform.

"Yes thank you, Starmol, and Pantol has fully recovered too." Archie sat down in the chair Starmol indicated.

"Oh yes," she paused. "The dragon."

Archie thought quickly. "Please don't even think of punishing him. He was only carrying out my request for assistance."

"How did you know your sister was here? Did Pantol tell you?" asked Starmol as they walked up a flight of steps to the Controller's office.

"Certainly not!" Archie was most annoyed on Pantol's behalf. "My sister Emmaline and I are twins. We have always known when the other is in trouble." Archie realised his bond with Pantol was in danger of discovery, and quickly related the swimming pool story to Starmol, who listened attentively.

"I was flying on Pantol, when I could feel that she was in desperate trouble and needed my help, so I asked Pantol to take me to her."

"How did you know where she was?" Starmol was interrogating him, Archie thought.

"That's easy. I could tell she was in a terrible state, and guessed she must have followed me here. Of course I realised you would have no use for another female."

Starmol gasped in surprise. "Why would you think that?"

Archie answered scornfully, "I'm not stupid, Starmol. Anyone could see you're already an all female society, where everyone knows her place.

My sister would not be likely to fit in with your plans at all, so I knew she would probably be dumped not too far from her arrival point. I remembered it was near the Rearer's houses, so that's the first place I asked Pantol to go.

You know what happened after that." Archie sat back and waited.

Starmol seemed uncomfortable, twisting in her chair.

"Where are my friends, Findley and Murray?"

"You know about Murray being here too?" Starmol was shocked.

"Why act so surprised, Starmol? He is my stepbrother. I know he was somewhere in the cottage when we accidentally found the time funnel.

My sister lives with him, so it would be no surprise to me to find they followed us here together. Didn't they?" he demanded, leaning towards her.

"Did you think you could keep him here without anyone knowing? We may have come from a time many years back in the past, but we are far from innocent."

"You don't understand…" Starmol began.

"But I do, Starmol. I understand only too well. I know that some of you want to introduce males back into your lives and some disagree. Which side are you on?"

"I am Controller. I cannot take sides. I have to ensure that nothing disrupts our lives whilst I am in charge." she sounded unsure, and Archie was quick to take advantage.

"Look," he urged her. "Just let me collect Murray and Findley, from wherever you've got them holed up, and we'll go straight back on the shuttle to the funnel, and no-one will be any the wiser."

"I wish it was that simple," Starmol sighed. "I'll take you over to Ring Three, where it will be easier to show you rather than explain here." she got to her feet and went to the door. Archie followed her.

"Ring Three? That's Hospitals, Life Planning and Reproduction, isn't it?" he asked as they walked together down the steps to the platform..

"Yes," Starmol said.

"Is that where you've got them captive?" he demanded.

"We are not barbarians, Archie. Nobody has captured anybody."

"Where are they then?" he asked as he settled into the shuttle. "I can't contact either of them. Have you locked their brains again?"

Starmol ignored him.

"Ring Three. Forward," Starmol said.

"Starmol! Don't go to sleep!" Archie said quickly, as she leaned back.

"I'm not!" she replied, startled. "Listen to me, Archie. Your arrival in our dimension has caused our people to look at their lives here with new eyes.

Unfortunately there is among us a faction of ten or eleven people who are not content to wait for nature to take its course. They are all for kidnapping and keeping suitable boys to bring up here in our ways."

"How can nature take its course without males?" Archie wondered.

"Well," Starmol sounded embarrassed. "We were rather hoping that Findley could help us with that."

"Just a minute," Archie had just realised what Starmol had said. "Have those renegades grabbed Murray and Findley? Is that why I can't contact them?"

"No, I don't think they would do that…"

"Are they the people who put Emmaline in that cage? What are you doing about it?" Archie demanded angrily.

"They will be punished, obviously. Things are a little difficult at the moment, but I do not believe they are particularly worried about your friends. It seems they have established another funnel down to your dimension. Well," she corrected herself.

"It is the same funnel, but it splits into two. Hyeke told us there is a small branch off the funnel on the way down. She and Bettina were following Pantol when they noticed it. We believe it comes out not far from your entrance."

Archie thought about it for a moment. "I bet it's that new house! I knew there was something strange about it. That noise I heard when I delivered the paper was just like the humming here. I wonder if they used the School Future Project as a way to disguise what they are after?"

"The School Future project?" asked Starmol. Archie explained.

Starmol agreed. "I'm afraid it does seem likely. We don't know for sure, but we believe they have already brought two boys back here. We have been told they are hidden in one of the Rearers' homes."

"They must be from the school. It's all my fault, I should never have come to this place!"

"It is not your fault, Archie. The funnel was there whether you used it or not. I suppose it was only a matter of time before they took things into their own hands. However, if they insist on capturing more people to bring here, they will find themselves in deep trouble."

"What will you do?"

"I shall have to enlist the help of the Overall Controller of Artross, but that will take time, and the link to your dimension may not last that long."

"I thought you said you had sole charge?" Archie scoffed.

"I do. As Controller of Wheel Trell I can do almost anything, but we all answer to the Overall Controller of Artross. She will not allow this. They must be stopped. What they are doing is completely wrong."

"How will you stop them? Will there be a fight? What can you do?"

"Fight? Why should we fight? We will advise them that their actions are unnecessary, now that you are here."

"Me?" Archie was worried.

"You and your friends," Starmol smiled.

"We know you can help us with a small donation of your seed, or even some of your DNA. Our scientists will do the rest. Introducing males into our society is not a problem. We can do it easily. No, our real problem now, is to decide whether we really want to re-introduce males into our lives."

"What?" Archie was shocked. "Why wouldn't you?"

"Believe me, Archie there are many reasons. You only have to look at your own Dimension to see the evil that men do. Not just to each other, to women and children too, and as for the planet, well, you know what is happening to your Earth."

Archie thought he could see what Starmol was driving at.

"Some of our people do not want to change what has worked so very well for so many centuries. They believe men may feel that they should control, or fight, or even subjugate women.

When humanity began, men needed to be aggressive for survival, but that is all changed now. Trell people are afraid the whole wars scene could start again, and all our work will have been for nothing," Starmol tried to explain.

"Are you?"

"Am I what?"

"Afraid?"

"I am Controller this week. I cannot have feelings."

"That's a copout. When is it somebody else's turn at being Controller?" Archie asked her.

"I have three days left before it is Brentolly's turn."

"Does this have to be resolved before then?" Archie asked, privately thinking of the months and months of discussion it would take in his dimension before the government took a decision.

"Yes. Any matter arising while I am Controller has to be dealt with before I leave. It's the rules."

"There is one matter you could change," Archie suggested. "Your custom of putting dying dragons into the Dying Chamber."

"What do you mean? I know you stayed there last night. It was very foolish of you."

"See? That is what I mean, why don't you try some lights, water, food and some kindness? It would make all the difference to the welfare of the sick dragons. You never know, some might just survive!" he said pointedly.

"You do not understand, Archie, we do not put them in there, they go in of their own free will."

"Only because there is nowhere else for the dragons to go without being a burden on their families, anyway that it not the point; what I am trying to say is ill animals would feel better if they were cared for in their last moments. Some heating perhaps, and some comforting words. Why are the Carers not allowed to stay? Bettina would not have minded staying with Pantol last night." he said. "I bet you don't put sick females in there, do you?"

"I told you, we do not *put* anyone or anything in there!" Starmol was getting cross.

"However, I believe I know what you are trying to say. I will give it some thought. Perhaps it wouldn't be such a bad idea after all. It would certainly be a good thing if there were more survivors. Everyone was very surprised to see that Pantol had made a complete recovery. Perhaps it was because he had your company. I suppose it would not be too difficult to change the Artrossian's attitude to the Dying Chamber. I know it is a most unpopular place."

"Thank you. Think of it as a testament to Pantol's bravery. He saved my sister Emmaline's life, you know, Starmol." Archie was very proud of Pantol, and was determined that some good would come of their frightening stay in the Dying Chamber.

"I know he did Archie, he was very brave." Starmol agreed. "All right, I agree. I will see that we change the rules. Now I have a more difficult problem to solve."

"Why don't you have a vote?" suggested Archie, "Surely something as important as this should have a consensus? Otherwise the next Controller who doesn't agree with you could change things."

"No," said Starmol, the Controller's decisions cannot be changed. That is why it is so important for me to get it right."

"Not all men are bad, you know, Starmol." Archie tried to persuade her." You could make certain they are all reared properly, with kindness and love."

"All our children are reared with love, Archie, our Rearers want their children. There is no question about that."

"You should not have to make such a decision on your own." Archie thought for a while. "Why don't you have a meeting and bring all the people together to decide?"

"The rules do not allow discussion. That is part of the reason our society is so successful. Everyone accepts the Controller's decisions. They know they have to, because when it is their turn, the people have to accept their decisions in their turn."

"So how are the Controllers elected?" asked Archie, as the shuttle doors opened, and he realised they had reached Ring Three.

"We are not elected!" laughed Starmol at the very idea. "We take it in turns.

Everybody, including the Rearers, over the age of twenty and under the age of thirty, is required to serve as Controller for one week.

It's not usually as difficult as it has been this week!" she added. "And it only comes round every couple of years or so."

The shuttle had come to a halt, and Starmol stepped down on to the platform, "Come on. It's just through here." she ushered Archie along the platform to large wide door, which opened as they drew near.

"This is the main Hospital." Just beyond the door there was the familiar biohazard curtain, which they passed through.

"I can't smell any disinfectant!" Archie thought. "The whole place smells so fresh and clean, and wow! Just look at these walls!" He admired the shining, clean, almost marble looking walls, which were so smooth and polished: the effect was to make it appear as if the corridor was lined with mirrors, making the whole place look light and airy. Archie glanced up and was astonished to see great swathes of green plants growing from holes in the walls, high above his head. He thought they couldn't be for decoration, they were too high up. "What is the green stuff?" he asked Starmol.

"They are oxygen plants. They breathe pure oxygen into the air. We have them in all our public places, and some smaller ones in our homes too." she told him.

"We have indoor plants at home as well," Archie remembered, "but I never thought of them as oxygen plants before."

"We do not use any chemicals or drugs here, or in our homes. We find our nano-technology, using proteins and phages to protect us much more adequately."

Starmol led the way through a corridor, and out into a large round foyer. A sign saying 'Reproduction' hung above a pair of white closed doors. Starmol approached a small depression at the side and placed her head in it. As her chin rested on the ledge beneath, the whole unit glowed, and with a click, the doors opened.

"Wow!" thought Archie. "What's that?"

"Face recognition," Starmol replied. "It goes down to the bones and teeth too, so nobody else can copy."

"They could cut off your head!" thought Archie.

"They would still be unable to enter, the unit can tell if you are alive by your eyes, and the pulses in your carotid artery."

Starmol laughed. "Come along, it's not far now."

Together they entered another foyer, and Starmol led Archie through a maze of rooms and corridors, and into a small white room. Eight tiny cots lined the walls, and nurses were washing, changing, and feeding the babies. They looked up as Archie entered the room, but relaxed and smiled as they acknowledged Starmol entering behind him.

"Wow!" said Archie. "They are so small." None of the babies were crying, even the babies waiting to be fed were quiet. "Are they alright? They are not making any noise or crying!"

"This year's set are, but we have been having a few problems recently. What we are desperately short of, is some new input to the gene pool," Starmol told him.

"Well, you could have been nicer to my sister, I'm sure she would have donated some of her DNA. Gene input doesn't necessarily have to be male, does it?" Archie asked her.

"Archie, you don't understand, we did not have your sister. If we had known she was here, we would have treated her differently. Unfortunately she was discovered by the renegades, before we could rescue her, and they as usual, act first, think last!"

"Why didn't Brentolly or Hyeke tell me that!" demanded Archie.

"Would you have listened?"

"I suppose not. Rebels! It's not just males who can be difficult then!"

"Yes, you do have a point there, Archie!" Starmol sighed.

"Where are the mothers?" he asked, wondering if they had mothers yet.

"The babies are only started in test tubes, Archie, they are then transferred to the chosen Rearers to be incubated and born normally," she laughed. "They're resting in other rooms, just down the hall."

"Oh!" Archie was relieved.

"Come on, let's go and find your friends." Starmol took his arm. They thanked the nurses, and apologised for disturbing the babies' routine, as they left the room.

They walked along the corridor, up some steps, along another corridor and out into a large glass conservatory. There were comfortable chairs set out around the room, and although it was quiet in there, Archie could hear a soft music in his head. It was unlike anything he'd ever heard before, and he immediately felt warm and relaxed, as he entered the large, glass enclosed space.

"Archie!"

Archie spun round and saw Findley entering the room behind them, followed by a young woman wearing a white tunic.

"They said you were here. What happened to you? Is Emmaline safe?" Findley said urgently. "I tried and tried to contact you but, somehow, my telepathy had stopped functioning."

"Hmmm. I wonder why!" Archie looked expressively at Starmol who had the grace to look embarrassed.

"I am sorry, I have reactivated your telepathic ability now Findley."

Findley blushed and shrugged his shoulders.

"Emmaline is okay. What about you, Findley?" Archie looked at his friend closely, and was amazed to see him blush. He caught a jumble of his friend's thoughts and immediately understood his friend's confusion.

Starmol smiled, and indicated the white robed woman "Archie, this is Wyntta. She says Findley has been very helpful." She turned to Findley, who fidgeted shyly. "We are all very grateful to you, Findley."

Archie could hear Findley's thoughts again, and realised Findley was embarrassed.

He grinned at him. "Okay, Findley?"

His friend nodded.

Archie turned and said to Starmol. "Now all we need is for you to bring Murray here and we'll be on our way; we need to find those boys and help them escape. You don't need us any more now, do you?"

Starmol was uneasy. "I'm afraid I have just heard some bad news, Archie. "Murray is in the hands of the renegades. I have informed the Overall Controller, but it will be three days before she arrives."

"What? In that case, we had better find him ourselves. Come on Findley."

"Wait a moment, Archie. How can we find him when we have no idea where he is being hidden." Findley objected.

"How many Rearers' houses are there? Starmol?" asked Archie. "They must all be searched. Can you organise that?"

"Yes, but all the Rearer's homes have stairs leading straight to the Ring road. They could take the boys anywhere, long before we could find them." Starmol told him.

"We are wasting time, talking. Is there a quicker way out of here?" Archie asked. "Show us how to get to Maintenance. Come on quickly!"

Wyntta pointed at a small door in the wall. "That will lead you straight back to the shuttle centre. Open." she commanded. The door opened at her request. Starmol and Archie hurried through.

"Now close the door behind us," ordered Archie to Wyntta as he went through, "and tell nobody where we are going."

Findley followed, and as he went through, Wyntta hugged him and thanked him again for his help, and added quietly, "Imagine Findley, you will know, that whatever happens in your time, your line will still survive thousands of years into your future!"

"Scary!" said Findley, embarrassed all over again. "Bye Wyntta!" and as she closed the door quietly behind him, Findley hurried to catch up with the others.

They all ran as fast as they could down the tunnel, Starmol leading the way and Findley, panting, bringing up the rear.

"Why are we going to Maintenance Archie?" asked Findley. "Shouldn't we be heading for the Rearers' houses?"

"If we can stop the roads, and the shuttles, there should be no way the renegades can get off the Ring. It will slow them down, and give us a chance to find the boys." Archie said as they reached the shuttle.

"Maintenance should be able to shut everything down. Am I right Starmol?"

"Yes. That's good thinking Archie."

They quickly got to their seats, and as the cushions wrapped them safely, Starmol said,   "Maintenance. Forward."

Moments later, they arrived and hurried after Starmol as she led the way. She ran up some steps, arriving at a closed door. She quickly set her chin on the ledge underneath another face recognition machine set into the wall. After a few seconds, the doors opened, and they went inside.

"It's lucky I am Controller this week," she said. "Nobody but myself and the engineers are allowed in here."

Archie and Findley stared round the huge room in astonishment. The whole place was completely covered in walls of screens, with differently coloured lights blinking everywhere. All the screens were being monitored by engineers, busy pressing buttons on their consoles, or talking at the screens.

On one wall directly in front of the boys was a giant map of Rings and Shuttle connections. The whole transport system of Wheel Trell was laid out before them.

Chapter Nine

Archie to the Rescue Again

"Where is the Chief Engineer?" asked Starmol. "This is an emergency!"

An older woman, dressed in an all in one set of crisp, clean overalls, slowly came forward, eyeing the boys with suspicion. "This is a Top Secret Area." she pointed at the boys "These people do not have Clearance to be here. Who are they?" Archie could hear her ask Starmol, and he heard her answer.

"Hesta. I do not have time to explain right now. The renegades have captured and hidden some of their friends. We need to find them fast, before the link to their time fades."

"What do you expect me to do? Help you look for them? They need to leave. Now!"

Hesta was not troubling to hide her disagreeable thoughts from them and her unhelpfulness came as a nasty shock to Archie.

Starmol was firm. "We need you to shut off all the shuttles. Please do as I say, now! None must get to the outer Ring. We have to search the homes."

"Just give us time to get there first," thought Archie. "Please," he added as he felt Hesta hesitate.

Findley had been watching the screens.

"Hey!" he called." Look!" They all swung round and watched the blinking lights of a shuttle slowly departed from the outer ring.

"It's coming from the Rearers' section. Stop that shuttle now!" ordered Starmol.

"I can't do that!" Hesta argued. "They might be perfectly innocent."

"Then they've nothing to worry about. Now we're going to shuttle up to their next stop. When we arrive, pull that shuttle in behind us."

"In the meantime," Archie added, "You'd better stop all shuttles except ours until we can find the other boys."

"Who do you think you are? Giving me orders?" Hesta put her beefy hands on her hips, "I'll have you know I am in charge here, and no-body tells me what to do!"

"Except me." Starmol said to her quietly. "I want you to do just as he says, Hesta. If we don't find them, I will lead us on to the outer Ring. Then Hesta, you must close all shuttles down between Ring Seven and Eight.

I will let you know when to proceed as normal. If the people travelling in from the Outer ring are legitimate, we will swap shuttles so they can continue on their way, and we will take their transport back to the Rearer's homes."

Leaving Hesta with a scowl on her face, but no time to argue, Starmol hurried the boys out of the door. They ran back to the shuttle, and boarded quickly. Starmol ordered it to move along to Ring Six.

Findley was anxious. "Suppose the boys don't want to come?" he asked Archie.

"Are you kidding? Don't be a nerd, Findley. When we tell them there's no chance they'll ever get home again, they're not going to argue." Archie told him crossly. "And don't even think about asking them if they want to stay, Starmol," he added.

"Oh, no Archie. I agree with you. It would be entirely wrong to take advantage of
them like that."

"Good." Archie sat back.

The shuttle drew into the platform and the doors opened. Starmol went along to the
next shuttle which sat waiting a little way up the tunnel. "Open!" she commanded the
doors. As they slid open Archie and Findley were disappointed to see two women and a small girl standing at the door, looking anxious.

"Thank Goodness!" the older woman exclaimed. "We thought we were stuck. What's happening?"

"Sorry for the inconvenience." said Starmol. "We have lost some of the boys who gained access to Artross through the time funnel, and as this shuttle has just come from the outer Rings, we felt they may be aboard."

"Boys! The ones captured by the renegades, do you mean?"

"Yes," answered Archie quickly "Have you seen them?"

"No, but we heard them!" The woman grinned as she said, "Until they shut off their thought transference."

"Are they all right?" demanded Starmol.

"They didn't seem to be too happy about where they were being held. Something about it being dark, and the door was locked."

"Right. Thanks," said Starmol "You can carry on in the next shuttle. It will take you on your way. Sorry for the delay."

Archie waited until the woman and the girls had boarded the other shuttle, and it had moved off, before turning to Starmol and Findley, his face alight with excitement.

"I know where they are being kept!" he pulled at Starmol's arm. "Come on! Let's take this shuttle to the Outer ring. Quickly!"

They all jumped into the shuttle, sat down and waited while Starmol ordered the vehicle "Move Forward".

Findley was the first to notice. "Hey!" he shouted, forgetting to use telepathy. "We're not moving. Look!"

They all looked up at the map on the ceiling. Sure enough, the little flashing light was not moving, indicating that the shuttle was still stationery.

"It's Hesta," thought Archie angrily. "She's deliberately delaying us, to give them time to escape. I knew there was something about that woman I didn't trust."

Starmol was horrified. "Oh no, Archie. I'm sure you're wrong."

"Why are we still sitting here then?" argued Archie. "Come on Starmol, is there a way to Outside from here?"

"Yes. We can use the auto stairs, but why do you want to go Outside?" puzzled Starmol.

"I'll tell you on the way. Come on," Archie said.

Starmol gave the command to "Open" and for one heart-stopping second, they thought they had been locked in, but the doors opened slowly,

"No, even Hesta isn't that brave!" Starmol thought.

They ran to the steps after Starmol, and grabbed the safety rails, as she said aloud

"Outside." The stairs flew upwards so fast they nearly fell over. When they reached the top, they stepped out onto a wide path. Starmol told them it went right around the outside ring, but it was used so rarely that it was never converted from static to rolling, so they would have to walk.

All was quiet as they went out and looked about. There were very dark clouds gathering and a warm wind was blowing.

"We are still some way from where we need to be," Starmol worried. "The Rearers' houses are a long way over there. And this wind means a storm is coming."

"Good. That means there won't be anybody about outside," thought Archie.

Findley asked, "Archie. How do you know where the boys are?"

"Well, I might be wrong, but there is only one place I know about near the Rearers' homes that is dark inside, the way that woman described, and that's the Dying Chamber."

"Yes, of course. That would be the very place. Nobody would think of looking in there." Starmol agreed.

Findley raised his eyebrows, querying: "Sounds pretty gruesome!"

"Believe me, it is a horrid place. I spent last night in there, and if I had known what it was at the time, I would have had the heebie-jeebies, I can tell you!" said Archie feelingly.

"What were you doing in a Dying chamber Arch? How did you come to spend the night there?" Findley pressed.

"You might well ask, but it's a long story Findley. I'll tell you later. We should get going now. Hesta will probably warn the rebels. Come on, which way Starmol?"

"We should be able to find one of the farm lanes to follow. There are several, all round the Ring entrances."

"Of course, that will be how the farmers get their produce to the maitre'd." Archie added anxiously. "These clouds are very worrying. If it gets much darker we will not be able to see where we are going."

"Here!" whispered Findley, "I just thought, "Suppose the renegades can hear us?"

Starmol stopped. "What did you say Findley?"

Archie quickly explained about the whispering, and repeated what Findley had asked him. Starmol hurried to put his fears to rest.

"When I told The Artross Controller the names of the renegades, she put a block on them, so they hopefully will be unable to receive any thought transferences, except between themselves."

"Good, that should give us a bit more time, unless of course Hesta manages to pass them a message."

Starmol still could not believe Hesta would do such a thing and told the boys "Hesta values her position as Chief Engineer too much to jeopardise it. She knows what happens to traitors."

Findley was just about to ask what happened to traitors when Archie who was walking in front, put his hand up and said "Wait!"

"What is wrong Archie?" Starmol stepped alongside him, and tried to see in the gathering gloom.

"I don't know, but I think I saw something moving out there." He pointed away in front. "It was quite big. Could it have been a raptorvor?"

As they waited, watching for they didn't know what, they heard Findley suddenly shriek, from just behind them.

"For goodness sake Findley, keep quiet! Sound carries across ground like this." Archie was annoyed with his friend.

"Sorry, Arch. Something touched my arm. It made me jump!"

"Huh! I'll make you jump in a minute!" Turning to Starmol he said "Can you see anything, Starmol?"

"No, but it's as dark as night now and I think we should hurry down to the next Ring entrance before we are caught in this storm." She started to walk faster down the track, carefully following the trail of white stones that served as a guide at the edge of the lane.

Archie was keeping a sharp lookout as he hurried behind her. He was sure there were things out there. Dark shadows were following them. He began to think they would never reach the safety of the next Ring entrance.

The wind was picking up now, roaring and angrily snatching at their clothes, and he could see Starmol's hair streaming horizontally in front of him. So much for his hedgehog cut, that would be flat as a pancake!

He stopped and turned his head to make sure Findley was keeping up. The noise of the wind and the strange loud whistling of it in the stubby cereal crops, made it difficult to think. He walked backwards, trying to see his friend, but the wind stung his eyes and they streamed with tears. He couldn't see him at all now.

"Findley!" he stumbled and came to a halt. "Starmol, I can't see Findley!"

Starmol came hurrying back. "He must have fallen. Come on, he can't be far."

Together, they battled to keep upright in the wind, back the way they had come, until..

"There he is!" Archie ran the last few steps and bent down to his friend, who was lying crumpled on the ground, groaning.

"Sorry Arch. I think I've twisted my ankle."

"Can you stand?" Starmol knelt down beside Findley ran her fingers round the boy's ankle. "I don't think it is broken, but it is beginning to swell up. Better take your shoe off before it becomes too tight." She carefully unlaced his trainer and gently wiggled it off Findley's foot, which was fast turning black, and handed it to him. Findley stuffed the shoe in his pocket, groaning as together, Starmol and Archie lifted him to his feet, and each putting an arm round him, they started back down the lane, Findley hopping on his good foot, the winds now howling hysterically around them.

"It's as if the wind is alive, if it gets much worse, we will not be able to stand up. I'm finding it very hard as it is." thought Archie.

"Hey, you know what? It's a good thing, this thought transference. If we were trying to talk, we'd never make ourselves heard in all this noise. Could that be how it all started, Starmol?"

"Probably Archie, but I don't know. We have always been able to do it."

Findley let out a groan "Sorry, but I don't think I can manage to go much further."

They stopped to get their breath.

Starmol suggested "Let's sit down for a rest before the hail comes."

"Hail?" worried Findley.

"Yes, it always hails when it blows like this. We must find some shelter soon."

"Should we go back?" asked Archie.

"I think we are a bit nearer to the next entrance, but there is no way we can get there before the storm breaks. I am afraid we are going to get caught out in the open here. Soon it will be too difficult to go on, or back." she added,

"How are we going to get you to safety?" Starmol worried.

"Let me think for a minute." Archie was worried, he knew Findley could not go much further without help, and he hoped the dragon would forgive him for dragging him back into this mess. He had done enough already, but Archie could think of no other way out.

"Pantol," he sent the thought, safe in the knowledge that Starmol couldn't hear him.

"I need your help. Can you fly in the storms?"

Pantol's reply was instantaneous. *"We can at the moment, Archie, but not for too much longer. This is going to be a bad one by the look of it. It rarely gets as dark as this during the day. A few of my friends have been watching you to see that you made it back inside, but did not feel they could intrude."*

Archie grinned in relief to know the dark shadows hanging around behind them were friendly.

"I wish I had called on you earlier. Findley is hurt, and we need you and a couple of friends to come over to help, and we have some more rescuing to do!"

He felt the warm glow before his friend's voice filled his head.

"We are not far away, Archie, who needs rescuing now?"

Archie put Pantol in the picture and explained that they should just 'drop by' so

Starmol would not suspect the bond between them.

Pantol snorted. *"She's not stupid, Archie! It would be better to tell her. She's one of*

the good ones!"

While he waited for the dragons to arrive, Archie explained to Starmol that he had contacted Pantol, and he was on his way to their rescue with a couple of his friends.

She was amazed "How on earth did you get in touch with the dragons? Ahhh." She nodded. "So you super-bonded then?"

A bit shame faced, Archie thought "Yes. Sorry I didn't tell you."

"That's all right. How lucky you are. It never happened to me."

"What are you two on about?" Findley asked, exasperated with all the secrets.

"Tell you later!" Archie said airily. "Look. Here they come."

With a whoosh, three dragons dropped out of the sky at their feet, their feathers ruffling iridescently, the colours of rainbows in the fierce winds.

"Where do you want to go?" Pantol asked as Archie mounted him and watched Starmol and Findley settling themselves comfortably on the other two dragons.

"We need to go to the Dying Chamber, where they put us last night. The renegades have locked three boys up in there, to prevent them getting back home."

"I did not think we would be seeing that miserable place again so soon, Oh well, if we must, we must, the Dying Chamber it is then. Right! Ready?" The three dragons jumped up into the air and flew, slowly, trying to avoid being too badly buffeted by the wind, as it screeched and howled around them. Even with the protective cushions holding them tightly on the saddles, it was a huge relief to all of them when they sighted the small round houses in the distance.

Gradually, just as Archie thought they were getting a little too close to the Rearer's houses for comfort, the dragons began to slow down and one after the other landed gracefully on the grass outside the large black sinister looking wedge-shaped building that Archie remembered from the night before. When they had all dismounted, Findley looked around him.

"What is this place Archie? It looks pretty unwelcoming if you ask me."

"It's the Dying Chamber. You're right, it is a bit spooky. I stayed here last night with Pantol. Now everyone listen, please. This is important.

When we open the doors we will have to be as quick as we can. When the boys see us their thoughts will be picked up by the renegades and they'll know they are being rescued, so we don't have much time."

Starmol intervened: "I can help you there, Archie. I can block their thoughts altogether. Only for a few minutes, but it should give you time to get away."

She stepped forward and said, "Open." The doors opened and Archie and Findley could see three boys sitting on the mat on the floor. They looked up and rubbed their eyes as the unexpected light made them water. In the gloom, they hurriedly scrambled to their feet, shielding their eyes and trying to see who had opened the doors.

"Craig! What on earth?" Archie was astounded to see his older brother.

"Quickly," Pantol warned him. *"Explanations come later."*

Starmol pointed to two of the boys, "You and you get on that blue dragon, and you,"

she pointed at the third one, "mount up on the yellow one with Findley. Archie, you ride Pantol, he cannot carry two after his ordeal last night."

The boys fell over themselves to get on the dragons. Archie sat astride Pantol and

looked down at Starmol, worried for her safety.

"What about you?" he asked.

"Don't worry Archie, I am looking forward to confronting those rebels," she said.

"What will happen to them?" asked Archie.

"They will be exiled to another wheel, the same way we treat all traitors, and never allowed back. They will have to build new lives for themselves and their families, and they will be closely watched to see that they do. Go safely now, and hurry!" she urged. They didn't need telling twice.

The dragons took off and soared into the air. Soon Pantol and Archie could see the shimmering of the biohazard prevention covering the area around the hole leading to the funnel. Archie looked around. It seemed they had not been detected yet. He beckoned the others to follow. Quickly and silently, the dragons landed at the entrance. *"Hurry,"* Pantol thought urgently, *"I can hear followers."* The boys ran to the funnel and stepped in.

Archie threw his arms around the dragon's soft feathery neck.

"Wait till I tell my friends about you! They won't believe me. Thank you, thank you Pantol. See you." He stepped into the funnel behind the others.

- - -

Archie woke up in a very elegant sitting room where Findley, Craig, and Murray were anxiously waiting for him to come round.

"Oh my head!" he groaned, as he looked round, surprised to find he was not in the cottage. "Is this the house in Hearmian Lane?" he asked.

"Yes." answered Craig, surprised. "How did you know?"

"I just guessed. Where's the other boy?" he whispered.

"Mike. He's scarpered, didn't want to wait. What a wuss!" Craig helped Archie to his feet, "Hurry, we're going out of the French windows, and round the back. There doesn't seem to be anybody about, but we're not taking any chances of being caught."

The boys crept out of the doors like mice, and ran round the side of the house, through the large garden to the road, where they recovered their bikes.

"Hang on a minute," Archie said as they all began to get ready to ride off. "We should make sure no-one else knows about this place. You'll have to get Mike to keep quiet, Craig. It is very important. If he blabs, we'll have all and sundry trying to find the future funnels, and who knows what could happen."

"I'll do what I can. If he says anything, we'll all deny it and people will just think he's a bit mad. Let's face it Archie, nobody in their right mind is going to believe him, are they? By the way, we are all meeting at the school later to discuss what happened yesterday. I'll be sure to tell the boys not to let Mike give us away."

"Yesterday?" Archie looked at Craig. "What about yesterday? Oh yes. The School Future Project. I remember now. So? What happened?"

"Three women came to the school and said they were from the future. They were dressed in strange long tunics, but we thought they were just some actors dressed up and having a laugh."

"Three of the renegades." guessed Archie

"Yes, we know that now, but at the time nobody believed them. Anyway they told us if we went to their house, they would prove it, so for a laugh I asked Mike to come along with me, and they brought us here, to the house in Hermian Lane,"

Craig added. "It was quite extraordinary!"

Archie grinned, "Tell me about it."

Craig said crossly, "It wasn't at all funny Archie. They took us, Mike and me, up a sort of funnel to their time, and when we woke up we were in a huge barnlike place. It was very dark, and we had no idea where we were.

When we realised we had been locked in, we started calling for help, then we heard somebody else moving about near us, and discovered Murray was there as well. Then," Craig added in amazement, "You know what Archie, we found out that we could read each other's thoughts!"

"Yes," said Archie, "They unlocked some part of our brains, and that enabled us to communicate telepathically."

"We can't do it now, though." Craig said regretfully.

"I know," agreed Archie. "I think it can only happen in the ninth dimension."

"Ninth dimension?" asked Murray "Is that where we were? I couldn't understand how Craig and Mike got there, as well as me and Emmaline." he asked Archie.

"Do you know where Emmaline is, Archie? The women separated us when we arrived, and took her away somewhere else. I don't know where she is. I've been so worried about her. I know I should never have taken her with me. I haven't seen her since." he added anxiously.

Craig was still trying to make sense of it all. "Murray told us he was following you, Archie. There seem to have been two time funnels leading to the same place. Odd really. Anyway, it is a good thing you knew where to find us. How did you know, by the way?"

Not waiting for Archie's reply, Murray asked again, insistently,

"Archie? Do you know where Emmaline is? She was with me, when I looked through the window and saw you stand on the carpet and disappear. They took her away when we followed you, when we landed in the bubble. I hope she's okay."

Archie felt sorry for Murray, he knew he blamed himself, but if he knew his sister, Murray wouldn't have had any say at all in where she went. He smiled at his stepbrother.

"She's quite safe, Murray," he said, putting him out of his misery. "She'll be at Dad's waiting for news. I'll just check in with Mum, and then I'll come over and tell you all about it."

Later that night, after Archie had returned from his Dad's, he lay in his bed, wondering what Starmol was going to decide.

He thought he hadn't presented the case for boys very well. Perhaps he ought to go back. He'd like to see Pantol again. He smiled as he remembered the baby dragons.

He thought about the entrance to the funnel in the new house. The renegades had obviously strengthened it somehow. He thought he might just drop by next Saturday and see if it was still there, with the renegades sent to another Wheel, there shouldn't be anyone about to stop him. Smiling, he fell asleep, dreaming of dragons…

END

."